...ody country.

Branch:

DEMCO

The Bloody Country

by the same authors
My Brother Sam Is Dead

by James Lincoln Collier
Rock Star
The Teddy Bear Habit
The Hard Life of the Teenager
Inside Jazz
Why Does Everybody Think I'm Nutty?
Rich and Famous: The Further Adventures of
    George Stable

by Christopher Collier
Roger Sherman's Connecticut: Yankee Politics and
    the American Revolution
Connecticut in the Continental Congress

The Bloody Country

by James Lincoln Collier and
Christopher Collier

Four Winds Press   New York

Library of Congress Cataloging in Publication Data

Collier, James Lincoln.
  The bloody country.

  SUMMARY: In the mid-eighteenth century a family moves from
Connecticut to Pennsylvania and becomes involved in the property con-
flict between the two states.
  1. Wyoming Valley, Pa.—History—Juvenile fiction. [1. Wyoming Valley, Pa.—History—Fiction. 2. Pennsylvania—History—Fiction. 3. Frontier
and pioneer life—Fiction] I. Collier, Christopher. joint author. II. Title.
PZ7.C678Bl [Fic] 75–34461
ISBN 0–590–07411–3

Published by Four Winds Press
A Division of Scholastic Magazines, Inc., New York, N.Y.
Copyright © 1976 by James Lincoln Collier
and Christopher Collier

For Judith Whipple, Friend and Editor

The Bloody Country

I

*F*ather told me and Joe Mountain to go berrying up in the old Indian cornfield. They didn't use it anymore and it was full of raspberry bushes, and we knew it was time for them to be ripe. Mother didn't want us to go. "It isn't safe, Daniel," she said.

"There won't be any British troops back up there. They'll be coming down the river if they come."

"When they come," she said.

"Besides, they're not going to hurt a couple of nine-year-old boys," he said.

"They have Indians with them. You can't trust what those Indians will **do**."

"The British will keep them under control," Father said.

"There are a lot more Indians than British out there. At the fort they said there were seven hundred Indians and only four hundred whites."

"They aren't going to bother a couple of boys picking berries. Besides, Ben and Joe know the woods around here better than the British do. They won't have any trouble finding places to hide if they have to."

"I don't like it," Mother said.

But Joe and I wanted to go. We'd just as soon spend the day picking berries out in the Indian old field as stay around the mill. If we stayed home Father would make us do something hard, like carrying rocks for the dam. Out there in the berry patch we could sit around and talk as soon as we got our baskets full.

"We'll be careful," I said.

"How can you be careful of seven hundred Indians, Benjamin?" she asked.

"Don't worry about them," Father said. Of course, she couldn't go against Father, so she gave in, and Joe Mountain and I got berry baskets and left. It was a wonderful day, just so beautiful. The road from Wilkes-Barre went along the Susquehanna River, and an old Indian path led away from it through woods into the hills where the Indian old field was. The Indians used it to get to the Susquehanna River before there were any white people there. They used to put fish heads in the hills of corn for fertilizer, and they probably came down to the river to catch fish. There were plenty of fish in the Susquehanna all right—bass, trout, shad, perch, and more. They could use any of them to make the corn grow.

The path went upward. Everywhere there were birds dashing through the air, and sitting on the branches of the oaks, singing: blue jays, robins, flickers—I couldn't name them all. Squirrels would sit there and look at us, maybe chewing on a nut and then, when we got closer, drop the nut and race up a tree trunk.

"Do you think the British are going to come?" I asked.

"I'll fight 'em," Joe Mountain said.

"You wouldn't fight the Indians, would you?"

"Sure, I would," he said. "I'm not afraid of Indians."

"You're an Indian yourself," I said.

"Hell, I'm not an Indian," Joe Mountain said. "I'm a nigger."

"The hell you aren't," I said. "Your mother was a Mohegan."

"She wasn't any real Indian, she was just a regular

mother. Besides, if I'm not a nigger, how come I belong to your father? Indians can't be slaves, only niggers."

We got Joe Mountain a little while before we came out to Wilkes-Barre from Windham, the town where we used to live in Connecticut. Joe Mountain's mother was an Indian. She lived in a hut up back of Colonel Dyer's house. She didn't belong to Colonel Dyer or anything; I guess he just let her live there. Colonel Dyer had a nigger slave named Joe, and he got to be the Indian woman's husband, and Joe was born. Then Joe's mother got cholera and died, and there was nobody to take care of him, so Colonel Dyer sold him to my father. I guess Father didn't actually pay anything for Joe. Colonel Dyer owed him some money for some land or something; I don't know exactly what it was. Anyway, I was glad we got Joe. It gave me a friend. It gave me somebody to talk to when we were working. I figured it was better for Joe, too. I figured it was better to live with a miller than in an Indian hut, even if you had to be a slave. Although it seemed funny to me that he was a slave if he was an Indian. "Well," I said, "I guess the part of you that's a nigger is a slave."

"How come the rest of me isn't free?"

I didn't know the answer to that. It bothered me some. If Joe Mountain was only part nigger, he ought to be part free. I mean maybe he could be a slave in the mornings and free in the afternoon. "Maybe Father will set you free some day."

"Oh, sure," he said.

"Well, I'll set you free when I inherit you, Joe." But I didn't know if I would. The whole thing was a problem to me. There wasn't anything wrong with having a nigger slave. Lots of people had them. According to Father it said in the Bible that niggers were supposed to be slaves. But it bothered me to think that I could grow up and own the mill, or even become a sailor or a mason or whatever I wanted, and Joe would have to go on working for Father or me or whoever owned the mill for the rest of his life. But I didn't care what he said about his mother being an ordinary mother. She was an Indian all right. She had goats living in her hut. He was named after her. Well, I mean the name of Mountain wasn't really Mountain, it was some Indian name that sounded like Mountain. He got called Joe because that was the name of his father.

We went on up the path, scaring the jays and the squirrels. It made me laugh to see the squirrels stare at us and then drop their nuts and run up a tree.

"What's funny?" Joe asked.

"Nothing," I said. "It just makes me feel funny to see the squirrels race away like that."

"If I had a gun I'd shoot one," he said.

"I wouldn't let you."

"You couldn't stop me."

"The hell I couldn't."

"The hell you could."

I threw down my basket and charged at him. He jumped on me and we fell onto the ground and began wrestling. I was on top and he began squirming around trying to get his legs around me in a scissor grip. I rolled over to get free. "Hey, watch out, you're breaking my basket," he said.

I let go and kneeled up, and then he sat up; there was an Indian standing over us, just staring down at us. He was wearing homespun trousers and a red British army coat. There was a long knife in his belt and he was carrying a musket draped kind of easy over his arm. He was just about five feet away.

"Oh, God," Joe Mountain whispered. We stared at him and he stared back. Then he jerked his thumb to make us stand up. We stood up. He pointed up the trail toward the berry field and we began to run, feeling weak and scared and our hearts going as fast as the millstone. The Indian jogged along behind us. When we didn't go fast enough to suit him he poked us in the back with the gun. We went on up the path toward the clearing where the berry patch was. It was two miles, but the Indian made us run the whole way. It wasn't anything for him to jog a couple of miles but we weren't used to it, and by the time we were halfway there we were soaked in sweat and our mouths were twisted and gasping for air. But he didn't care, he kept on running us. Then suddenly we came into the clearing.

It was full of Indians, just sitting around. There were a few British redcoats there, too, but mostly it was Indians. They had guns and knives and tomahawks. I tried to count them, but when I got up to fifty I stopped. There was at least a hundred of them, and who knew how many more there were in the woods around?

The Indian who had found us pushed us into the clearing toward a Britisher. He was wearing some sort of little sword and I figured he was the officer. The Indian said something to him in Indian talk. The officer looked at us. "Where'd you come from?" he asked.

"We were going to pick berries, sir," Joe Mountain said.

"I didn't ask that. I asked where you came from."

"From the mill, sir," I said. My voice was quivering so much I could hardly talk.

"Which mill?"

"Our mill, sir," I said.

"In Wilkes-Barre, sir," Joe said.

The Indian said something in Indian talk again. Then he took the knife out of his belt and sliced it through the air.

The British officer shook his head. "We haven't reached the point of killing young boys, yet."

The Indian sliced his knife through the air again. "Spy," he said in English.

The officer stared at us. "Oh come, you boys aren't spies, are you?"

"No, sir."

"No, sir. We were going to pick berries."

The Indian sliced the knife through the air again. "Stop that nonsense," the officer said. "This is supposed to be a civilized war, not a bloody Roman circus. Take them back down to that farm we burnt and hold them there for an hour. We'll be gone from here by then. It wouldn't matter that they've seen us."

The Indian put the knife back in his belt.

"It doesn't really matter what they report, anyway," the officer said. "There's nobody around here to stop us from doing what we want. All right, take them out of here."

The Indian jerked his head toward the other side of the clearing. Then he laid his hand on the handle of his knife. We began to trot off. When we got part way across the Indian old field the British officer shouted, "No nonsense, hear? If I discover you've sliced their throats, it'll go hard with you."

There was a path leading out the other side of the clearing through the woods. The Indian ran us along it. He just jogged easily behind us, but we had to run fast to stay ahead. We didn't dare turn around to look at him. We both knew that he would kill us on the slightest excuse and we didn't want to give him one. He might just kill us anyway just for fun, like they killed the Hadsals and some others up the river.

We ran on that way for fifteen minutes and then the woods ended and we came into a cornfield. The corn was a couple of feet high. I knew where we were —it was the farm of Bill Crooks. I'd been there before, only we'd come by way of the road instead of through the woods. Out in the middle of the cornfield there used to be a house and a barn, but they weren't there anymore. Instead there was just a big patch of gray ashes with smoke still coming up from it.

We stood there catching our breath. Then the Indian said something in Indian talk and we started to run across the cornfield toward the smoking ashes. We ran down between the rows of corn, trying not to break any of the stalks. In a couple of minutes we come out of the cornfield into the Crooks's yard. We stared at the patch of ashes. I could feel the heat com-

ing out of it on my face. It was really burnt. There
was hardly a whole board or beam. Everything was
charcoal and ashes, with just here and there a piece
of something that could have been a table leg or part
of a bed sticking up out of the mess.

Somewhere in the middle of the pile there were
still a few flames, which flickered up a bit when the
breeze blew, and gave off an awful smell. I watched
the flames, and after a minute I realized that they
were flickering around a long shape. I went on looking at the shape and a cold chill began to grow across
my back, because I knew that the shape was one of
the Crooks boys. If you looked carefully you could
make out his face, sort of. I mean you could see his
teeth with no mouth around them and a kind of
black lump where his nose had been. I turned away
and threw up, and just when I stopped I heard a gag-
ging sound and I knew that Joe Mountain was throwing up, too.

The Indian shoved us away from the house toward
a maple tree that had shaded the south side of the
house, when there had been a house there to shade.
He pushed us down onto the ground, and made us
sit with our hands on top of our heads. He sat down,
too, with his legs crossed, the way Indians sit. He laid
the gun across his lap and took the knife out of his
belt, and tested the edge. Then he picked up a stone
from the dirt and began working on the knife edge.

"Maybe we better make a run for it, Joe," I whispered.

"I'm too scared," he said.

"Me, too," I said.

The Indian looked up at us and said something in Indian talk, and we shut up. Our arms were beginning to get tired from holding them on our heads. The Indian went on sharpening the knife with the stone and testing it with his finger. Every minute or so he looked up at us, and then went on sharpening the knife. Finally he was satisfied. He threw the stone out into the cornfield. Then he stood up and said something in Indian talk. We didn't understand him. Suddenly he jumped forward, grabbed Joe Mountain by the hair and jerked him upward until only the tips of his toes were dangling on the ground. "I'm an Indian," Joe shrieked. "Don't kill me, I'm an Indian."

I tried to run but my feet were stuck to the ground. The Indian laid his knife on Joe Mountain's throat. "Please, please," he screamed. The Indian pressed his thumb on the back of the knife. Joe's eyes were closed and his mouth was open, screaming. Then the Indian dropped Joe, put the knife in his belt, and trotted off across the cornfield. In a minute he was in the woods and out of sight. Joe and I began to cry and then we started for home along the road, walking and running and crying all the way.

2

When there was so much wilderness in America, more than anybody could ever measure, it's a queer thing that Americans would end up killing each other over it. I mean out beyond the Wyoming Valley where we lived there were millions and millions of acres of land in places like Kentucky and west of the Ohio, clear to the Mississippi River. It was good land, too, or at least that's what the mountain men who trapped out there said. There wasn't anybody living there except Indians, and not many of them either. You could buy land from the Indians cheap. So what was the reason for people killing each other over one little piece of a whole big country? But that's what happened.

Oh, you'd have understood it if it was only the white people against the Indians. The Susquehanna Company, which we were part of, had bought all of the land in the Wyoming Valley from the Indians years before, but the Indians hadn't kept to the agreement. They said it wasn't fair deal; or we'd bought it from the wrong Indians; or something, I never did get the idea of it. But whatever it was, the Indians had been causing trouble in the valley off and on ever since the Susquehanna Company bought it way back in 1754, before I was born. So you could understand if it was us and the Indians killing each other. And you could have understood it, too, if it was us against the British. I mean we were at war with the British and killing was part of that. But it didn't make any sense for Americans to fight each other—us Connecticuters against the Pennamites, which is what the people from Pennsylvania were called.

Every once in a while I'd ask Father to explain it to me again, and he always would, but it was pretty complicated and there was a lot of it I couldn't understand. It had to do with grants King Charles had given out to some Connecticut people a hundred years before. The Wyoming Valley is really in Pennsylvania, so you would think it would belong to

Pennsylvania. But it didn't, according to those old grants—it belonged to Connecticut. So around 1750—I don't know if that's exactly the right date—some Connecticut people formed the Susquehanna Company, and bought up all of the Wyoming Valley from the Indians who were supposed to own it, although I guess maybe they were wrong about it. And a lot of people joined the company and decided to come here and settle. But that made a lot of Pennsylvania people mad. They said the old grants didn't mean anything anymore; the Wyoming Valley was part of Pennsylvania and us Yankees from Connecticut had no business out here. And so it went, back and forth. There was a little fighting out here, but nothing too serious, and by and by we Yankees took over and began clearing the land and planting our fields and building our houses and barns. And everything seemed peaceful. But the Pennamites didn't just forget about the whole thing. They hadn't been able to drive us out, but they kept taking it up with the Pennsylvania courts or the Governor of Connecticut or the King in England. They didn't forget about it at all.

I guess if the Wyoming Valley hadn't been such a beautiful place the Pennamites wouldn't have minded that all of us Connecticuters were claiming it, but it really was a wonderful place to live. There was the Susquehanna River running through it, and lots of smaller rivers as well, like Mill Creek where our mill was. The woods were just full of game—deer and elk and even bear—and the rivers were jammed with fish. It wasn't any trouble at all to catch them. And depending on the season, ducks and geese and pheasant, too. And the forest was so beautiful—full of elms and maples and oaks with huge spreading branches, all clear underneath so that it wasn't any trouble to walk through the woods at all. But the main thing was the soil. All along the Susquehanna there were flood plains—flat places where the water left rich soil, and hardly any trees growing, so you could practically just come there and start plowing. Coming from Connecticut where the trees were practically all gone and the soil was worn out and stony and not so good for growing things anymore, it was like coming to Heaven.

We had been out in the Wyoming Valley for four years. Father thought about it a long while before deciding. I mean moving your whole family two hundred miles out in the wilderness is a pretty big thing. There were a lot of problems to it. First Father had to get the money to pay the Susquehanna Company for the land. Then there was the question of what we would do for a living out there. Father wasn't a farmer, he was a miller. I knew he was proud of being a miller instead of an ordinary farmer, although he never said so; it wasn't right to admit being proud of something like that, even if it was true. And then there was saying good-bye to all of my cousins and uncles and aunts and not seeing them again for years or maybe never.

But there were a lot of reasons for going, too. Already we had to travel nearly a mile to cut wood for the fireplaces and pretty soon that woodlot would be empty and we'd have to go even farther. Then there was the whole thing about the land going bad. A lot of the farmers had left and every year there was less grain for Father's mill to grind. A lot of others had given up growing grain and were just grazing sheep. It seemed like in time maybe there wouldn't be enough work for the mill to support us, and Father would have to go to work for my uncle John—that was Father's brother—and never be anything but a hired man for the rest of his life.

Father just couldn't stand the idea of that. He had a saying, "If you don't own your own land, you can't be your own man." It was a sort of poetical way of putting it, but I guess it was true. He said he knew of rich farmers who took their tenants down to the town meeting and told them how to vote. He used to say that a hired man wasn't any better off than a nigger slave—he had to do what somebody else told him all day; he might not even be able to get married and raise a family, but of course Father already had a family and didn't have to worry about that. Mother used to say that Father was too independent-minded for his own good sometimes, but it seemed to me that Father was right. Who wants to be a nigger slave to your own brother?

So he talked about it and thrashed it over with Mother for a long time—a couple of years, I guess. And then our millstream began to dry up. As long as there were woods along the streams, the rain would kind of soak slowly into the ground and seep into the streams and creeks gradually, so they'd run pretty steady all the year round. But when the farmers began cutting off the woods along the creek banks the rain water would rush into the creeks full force, and race away down to the ocean, tearing up the banks as they went. Then the creeks would dry up until the next rain. And so we began to have trouble with the creek the mill was on. There'd be plenty of water in the spring, but by midsummer it'd be so slow that it'd hardly turn the mill wheel. When he saw that happening, Father knew that it was time to go. Luckily, just at that time somebody from the Susquehanna Company came and said that some Indians had got into the mill in Wilkes-Barre and had stolen a lot of tools and burnt it. The miller didn't want to

stay there anymore, he said he was sick of Indian
trouble and sick of squabbling with the Pennamites,
he was coming back to Connecticut. Of course they
needed to have a mill in Wilkes-Barre, and they were
willing to give Father forty acres and sell him a lot
more land cheap if he'd go out there and start a mill.
And so Father decided to go.

So we packed everything into wagons—the two big
millstones and the mill irons and the tools, and our
chickens, and our furniture and clothes and everything, and traveled out to the Wyoming Valley.
There was Father and Mother, and me and Joe
Mountain, and my big sister Annie and her husband, Isaac. We had one millstone in each cart and I
used to sit on one of them because it was high up and
I could see around. We traveled through Connecticut and then into New York and across the Hudson
River and finally into Pennsylvania. As we went the
land changed. In Connecticut, where so much of the
woods had been cut off, you could see from the hill-
tops for miles—nothing but fields of corn and cows
grazing and houses here and there with thin lines of
smoke standing up from their chimneys. But then as
we got across the Hudson it was less settled. There
were more woods; sometimes we'd travel for miles
along a cart road with nothing but woods around us.
And when we finally got to Pennsylvania it was all

woods—just great oaks and elms and maples all around, with their branches so high sometimes that you could drive the carts right across the forest floor through the trees as if it was all one big road. There were birds everywhere, yellow and red and black, winging from tree to tree around us, and all the time tweeting and twittering. And, of course, there were chipmunks and squirrels and foxes, and sometimes we would see a herd of deer suddenly flash through the woods in front of us, just a quick dash and they were gone. Every once in a while we'd come to an old Indian clearing, where they'd had a field of corn. There'd be rabbits in the field who'd scatter as we came through, and once we even saw a bear standing at the edge of a clearing eating some berries. Father got a shot at him, but the bear heard us and jumped out of sight.

To me it was like Heaven. We had some woods in Connecticut, in the swamps or on the steep western faces of the hills that you couldn't farm anyway, but they weren't like the Wyoming Valley. Around Windham the deer were gone, the bears had been gone since my grandfather's time and there weren't any colorful birds, either—just the crows that came to eat the corn.

So that's how it was when we came to Wilkes-Barre. Father's land was at a beautiful place. The

Susquehanna came down through the valley from the north, maybe two hundred yards wide. On the east side there was a creek which ran pretty fast down a little hill over a rocky bed. Where the creek ran into the river was our land. We built a dam at the bottom of the creek, about fifty yards up from the Susquehanna, to make a little millpond, and we built our mill next to the pond. At first we lived in the mill, but then we built a house for ourselves, higher up onto the hillside and farther back from the mill creek than the mill was. Naturally, the mill had to be right beside the creek, but we wanted the house back a ways in case the creek overflowed its banks some spring. Then even farther up the hill we cleared off the woods and made a meadow. We had a cow for milk and a pair of oxen—a miller needs oxen to pull the grain wagon and to move rocks for dam building and a lot of other heavy work. The high meadow was a place for the cow and the oxen to graze.

On the opposite side of the creek from the mill was a steep, rocky cliff. A person could climb it easy enough, or skirt around it over the hill, but you couldn't get a cart over it. To go south into Wilkes-Barre it was easiest to go right along the bank of the Susquehanna; there was a wagon trail along there. We made a little dock on our side of Mill Creek, too, sticking out into the Susquehannah just where Mill

Creek went into it, so that farmers from across the river could bring their grain over by boat. It was, Father kept saying, "just a beginning." He had big plans worked out for expanding everything. "It's not like Connecticut," he would say. "We have a future here, Ben. A man can accomplish almost anything he can think up if he puts his mind to it, and doesn't object to a little hard work."

But the way it turned out, hard work wasn't going to be enough, because then came the Revolutionary War with the British. Oh, at first we thought it wouldn't have much to do with us. We figured the British would be more interested in capturing places like Philadelphia and New York than some tiny village like Wilkes-Barre. I mean what was Wilkes-Barre? Just about forty log houses and our mill, and a lot of farmers scattered around the countryside. Besides, some of our men had formed two companies of militia and they were ready to fight to protect us. But then our two companies got called to go to Valley Forge and when the British found out we hadn't any protection anymore, they decided to teach us a lesson. They joined up with a lot of Indians and started for us, and when the Pennamites saw what was happening, they realized that it was their chance to drive us out of the Wyoming Valley after all. So they began to march into the valley—British soldiers, Indians, and Pennamites. As they came they burned farms and killed the farmers who tried to fight them off. And it was that army that Joe Mountain and I bumped up against in the berry patch. It explains why we were so scared of them, too. We knew that they'd been killing people, and they didn't mind killing boys, either.

Of course, the next day we got over being scared and we went around boasting about how we'd been captured and almost killed. People heard about it and that afternoon some kids came up to the mill to hear the story. Joe Mountain began to make up stuff about it—how they'd tied us to a stake and tortured us. Well, I didn't like him hogging all the hero of it, so I said it was true, that they'd piled sticks around us and were going to burn us up like the Crooks boy, only I prayed to God and he sent over a rainstorm so they couldn't light the fire. Then Joe Mountain said that was how *I* got out of it but *he* got out of it because he told the Indians he wasn't really a nigger, he was an Indian and they let him go and were going to free him from being a slave and take him into the tribe, but just then the rain came and they were mad at not being able to burn me and they went away. Then somebody said that there hadn't been any rainstorm the day before, the sun had been out all day. So I said, well, God just sent the rainstorm right over where we were, and the kids began to say it was all lies but luckily my sister's husband Isaac came into the mill just then and made me and Joe sweep up the mill and chased the other kids away.

But it wasn't really funny. The British and the Indians were coming. Father and Mother had an argument about what to do. Father wanted us all to go up to Forty Fort, which was named after the first forty settlers who came to the area. Forty Fort was about a mile north, on the other side of the Susquehanna from us. We'd have to cross the river in our rowboat and walk up the other side.

Mother didn't want to go. "I don't like to leave the mill," she said. "As soon as it's empty Indians will get in and steal everything in sight."

"You've got a pregnant daughter here and two boys. We're better off up at the fort."

"They'll burn the mill for sure if we leave."

Annie's husband Isaac was in on the conversation, too. "They'll burn it down anyway if they decide to. Suppose Annie starts to have her baby when there are British around? There's no way to defend the place."

"Isaac is right," my father said.

"Well, all right," Mother said. "Annie and the boys can go up to the fort with Isaac. You and I'll stay."

Father shook his head. "No, Isaac will stay. You go up with the children."

She didn't like it, but Father had decided. Isaac

rowed us over and then we walked up to the fort.

It was pretty big, around seventy yards on each side. The walls were made of heavy logs with one end buried five feet into the ground. The wall was double thick, and built up against it on the inside were huts where people could live, or for storage. On each of the corners there was a sentry tower that went three feet above the walls. There was a four-pound cannon there, too, but it wasn't much use, because we had no shot for it. Forty Fort looked pretty strong to me, but the men there didn't seem to be so sure. We had only four hundred men and the British had a thousand, counting all those Indians.

The fort was pretty crowded, mostly with women and children. It sure was boring. There wasn't room enough to play any games. All we could do was sit around and talk. And worry. Although Annie and Mother were more worried than most. They were afraid that Annie would have her baby right there in the fort, maybe smack in the middle of some fighting or something. So for three days that's all we did—sit around and worry and watch the men drill, sort of marching back and forth. Father was one of the men; if there was fighting, he was going to have to fight along with the rest. It was kind of funny watching your own father march around like that with everybody else, doing right turns and left turns when the captain shouted out the orders. It was funny to see Father take anybody's orders. He wasn't much of an order-taking person.

Oh, my, we were bored. Me and Joe Mountain kept asking Mother if we could go home. "I'd like to go home myself," she said.

"When Father comes up to drill today, ask him."

"He won't agree," she said.

"Ask him anyway. Please."

"Please," Joe Mountain said.

But Father didn't come up to drill that day. "He had work to do no doubt," Mother said.

"I don't want to have my baby here," Annie said. "It's not right to have a baby in a fort."

"It isn't safe at the mill," Mother said. "The British are coming down both sides of the river and burning everything."

"Father and Isaac are at the mill."

"Somebody has to be there," Mother said. "But a pregnant woman and two boys aren't going to be much use to anybody."

"We can work on your garden."

Mother thought about that. She took a lot of trouble over her garden. She had cabbage growing there and peas and turnips and beans, and some herbs like thyme and bay. She even had some tobacco growing. She dried it and sold it in the winter to get money for needles and pans and other things she needed. Of course, Isaac begged about half of it from her. He liked to smoke a pipe. "Father and Isaac will worry about the garden," she said finally.

"I don't want to have my baby here, Mother. Not with all these men around."

"Be thankful for those men," Mother said. "Better to have them around than the British."

Suddenly Joe Mountain said, "We want to go home, too. We're bored."

"There's nothing to do here," I said.

"Being bored is better than being scalped," Mother said. But I could tell she was wavering. I knew she wanted to go home to look after her garden.

"We'll fight the Indians," Joe said. "We'll get some guns and fight them."

Mother just smiled.

"I'm not afraid of Indians," Joe said. "When those Indians captured us up in the old field I wrestled one of 'em down and took his gun."

"Oh, really," Mother said.

"I'd of killed him, too," Joe said, "only some other ones jumped on my back."

"Oh, Joe," Annie said disgustedly.

"That certainly was a lucky escape for the Indian," Mother said.

"There was a long bayonet on the gun and I was planning on stabbing—"

"Joe, be quiet," Annie said. "Mother, I'm not going to have my baby here."

She stared at her. "Well . . . ."

"I mean it."

She thought about it some more. "I really would like to have a look at my garden. I don't trust Dan and Isaac to do it. Well, all right, we'll go back for a visit, but we'll all come back tonight. Father will make us, that's for certain."

So we walked back down the river and waited until somebody was going over on a boat and could give us a ride. I always loved crossing the river. There was a big curve in the river there. It was about two hundred yards wide. You just sort of slid along through the clear water, watching the trees on the other side get bigger and bigger. The sun was warm and there was a little breeze which would ruffle the water in patches here and there. Oh, it was beautiful.

Father was angry with Mother for bringing us back. "It isn't safe," he said. "The British are everywhere and the Indians have been scalping people. Didn't you hear what happened to the Hardings at Jenkins Fort? They killed the whole family."

"It's just a visit, Dan," Mother said. "We're going back tonight."

"That's for certain," Father said. "All right, there's plenty of work to do. The boys can go do some hoeing in your garden just for a start."

Joe Mountain and I got out our hoes and went out to the garden. It was up above the mill, not too far from the creek, so it was easy to haul buckets of water for it during dry spells. It looked pretty bad; nobody had tended it since we'd been up at the fort. "Well, anyway," I told Joe, "it's better than being bored at the fort."

"We have to go back tonight," he said.

But we didn't go back that night and the reason was Annie thought she was having her baby.

3

*W*e were eating supper—just johnny-cake and gravy, because food was getting short, what with the British and Indians burning farms and slaughtering people's cattle to feed the troops with. But the johnnycake was good enough with hot gravy on it, and we were just digging in when suddenly Annie put her hand on her huge stomach and said, "Oh, oh, I think it's coming. I think it's coming."

"What does it feel like?" Mother asked.

"Like a tug," Annie said. "Like a pull."

"We'll see," Mother said. "No reason to take fright yet."

"I'm not going back to the fort if the baby's coming."

"Sometimes you think it's coming and it doesn't," Mother said. "It may be days yet."

"It came again," Annie said. "I felt it again." She got up from the table, and lay down on Mother and Father's bed, which was near the fireplace. She and Isaac had their own bed in the lean-to stuck onto the back of the house, but I guess she wanted to be where Mother was.

Mother laughed. "You may be lying there for a week."

Isaac frowned. "Don't joke, Mother," he said. "Maybe she's having it."

"Isaac, she knows best," Father said. "Leave it to her."

"Maybe she's having it," Mother said, "and maybe she isn't."

"I felt it again," Annie said. "I'm having it."

Isaac got up from the table, went over to the bed and knelt beside it. He didn't say anything, he just picked up her hand and squeezed it. "Mother, she can't go back to the fort until we see the outcome of this."

"We'll see," Mother said.

Joe Mountain and I were just as happy. With everybody worrying about Annie's baby it looked like we wouldn't have to go back to the fort right away. We cleared up the table after dinner, which was supposed to be Annie's job, but she was still lying on the bed explaining about the tugs and pulls to Isaac.

"I wouldn't be scared to have a baby," Joe Mountain said.

"Oh God, Joe," Annie said from the bed.

"I can't really picture it, Joe," Father said.

"All right," Mother said, "you boys outside. You too, Isaac. This is not for men."

She didn't tell Father to go, but he knew he should. He stood up. "I'll be in the mill," he said.

Isaac patted Annie's hand. Then he went outside and me and Joe went after him. We walked down to the Susquehanna, to the dock. We sat on the dock, looking at the sky begin to get dark and night come. Isaac had his pipe, and he filled it with tobacco and puffed some smoke around. The tree frogs were peeping, you could see bats wheeling the distances and there were mosquitoes buzzing around.

"Let us have a puff, Isaac," I said.

"It'll make you sick.

"It won't make me sick," Joe said.

"Me neither," I said. What Isaac didn't know was that me and Joe had our own pipe that somebody had left at the mill by mistake. We used to steal tobacco out of Isaac's pouch and smoke our pipe up in the woods where nobody could see us.

"All right," Isaac said. "Don't tell your mother, though." He gave us a puff and we sat there, listening to the water rushing along and the peepers and the mosquitoes humming.

"Do you think she's going to have her baby?" I asked.

"Your mother doesn't think so," Isaac said.

"I wonder what it feels like to have a baby," I said.

But then suddenly we were quiet, because we heard faintly in the distance the sound of a horse galloping. It was coming fast along the river road, being driven hard down toward us. Isaac knocked his pipe out into his hand and dumped the red ashes into the river, and we stood up and went back into the shade of the trees growing along the river, just in case it was British. He came riding hard and pulled up on the dock. I didn't know his name, but I recognized him: he was a farmer who used to come to the mill. We stepped out of the shadows of the trees.

"You folks better get the hell over to the fort," he said.

"What's going on?" Isaac said.

"They're only fifteen miles up river," he said. "They're coming down both banks. There's maybe a thousand of them—Indians, Redcoats, Pennamite Tories. They'll take anything they want, for sure."

He looked at me. "Is your father up at the mill?

"Run on up and tell him we're mustering at the fort. They want him right away." He looked at Isaac. "What about you?"

"My wife's having a baby," he said.

He shook his head. "Better get her up to the fort as soon as she can walk."

"Doesn't sound as if the fort'll hold," Isaac said. "Maybe people would be better off in the woods."

"Up to you," he said. He wheeled his horse around and raced off up the road.

"Let's go back to the mill," Isaac said. When we got there he made me and Joe Mountain wait outside in case Annie was having her baby. In a minute he came back out. "You can come in, boys," he said.

We went in. Annie was sitting in a chair, a blanket over her shoulders. "Did you have it?" Joe Mountain asked.

"It stopped," she said.

"They want you up at the fort, Father," Isaac said.

"All right," he said. "Let's go, everybody."

"I don't want to go," Annie said. "I want to stay here in case the baby comes."

"Annie—"

"I don't like it either," Isaac said. "I don't think the fort's going to hold. I'd rather see her out in the woods."

"And have her baby there?"

"Better off having her baby in the woods than in the middle of a battle," Isaac said.

Father stood there, thinking. Then he said, "Maybe. There's a lot of people out in the woods already."

"Father," Isaac said, "I think the best thing is for me to keep everybody here. Maybe the British won't come this way. Maybe they'll be too interested in Forty Fort and the other forts to worry about the mill."

"What'll you do if they come?"

"I'll put the boys up in the high meadow to keep watch. If they come this way, we'll go way up in the woods and hole up until it's over."

Father thought about it some more. Finally he said, "I think that's right. I don't like it, but I think it's safer. There's no telling what they'll do if they break into the fort."

So that was decided. Father took his musket and left; and Isaac went to get some sleep. Mother was going to stay up until midnight, and then Isaac would take over.

But nobody came that night, and Annie didn't have the baby, either. "It was just false labor," Mother said. "No wonder, with her being scared half to death all week."

Joe and I hoed in the garden all morning. The

land behind the house sloped up. The garden was higher than the house, just below the high meadow and we could see across the creek to the log houses of Wilkes-Barre pretty well. By the middle of the morning we knew we were in for something. There were people dashing around the village on horses, and a lot of boats going back and forth across the river—our own Connecticut men with their guns, women and children coming into the fort from the farms. A few of them were heading for the woods. One family came by us, just the mother and three children, and went off into the hills above the mill. They were scared and crying. Sometimes off in the distance we could hear shooting—a sort of rattle noise from the muskets and a deep boom when they fired the cannon.

But there was nothing to do but wait. At lunchtime Isaac told us to put away our hoes. "I want you boys to get up into the mill and keep a lookout." We went up there after we ate. The mill had three stories. First there was a cellar made of stone, where the gears and stuff were. We used it to store things, too, barrels of apples in the winter and lumber and baskets and bags for grain. Then there was the ground floor, where the millstones were. Finally there was a kind of loft where we could store corn and wheat before it was ground. We pulled the barrels of grain up there through a hole in the floor with a rope and pulleys. There was another hole there, right over the hopper above the millstones. You tipped a barrel over the hole, the grain poured out into the hopper and was fed into the stones. There were a couple of windows up there. Of course they didn't have glass in them; it was too hard to get glass out there without breaking it. From up there we could see way up the river to Forty Fort on the opposite bank. "Keep a good watch," Isaac said. "I don't want you fooling around."

But he didn't have to tell us that, because we were both good and scared. There was going to be fighting and people getting killed, that was for sure. Father was going to be in the fighting. I was scared that he would get killed. I wondered what it felt like to get killed. Or they might burn the mill or try to kill us. The British didn't kill women and children, that was their rule, but sometimes the Indians or the Tories did anyway, even though the British didn't want them to. I wondered what I would do if I saw somebody get killed. I wondered if I would faint or throw up again.

So we sat up there in the mill loft, each of us at a different window. The air up there was full of dust the way it always is in mills, and it was hot up there. We were sweaty and scared and the dust stuck to our sweat and made us itch.

It got to be late in the afternoon, and we began to hear drums off in the distance, coming from the fort. Then after awhile we could see the Connecticut men marching out. That far away you couldn't make out who anyone was. You could just about see the column and tiny flags going in front. I knew that Father was there somewhere, and a chill went up my back.

"I wish I was going to fight," Joe Mountain said.

"I'd be scared," I said.

He didn't say anything for a minute. Then he said, "Well, I'd be scared, too."

"Why do you wish you were going if you'd be scared?"

"I don't mind being scared," he said.

"I'd carry the flag," I said. "They don't shoot the ones who carry the flag, do they?"

"They shoot 'em first," Joe said. "If they capture your flag you have to surrender."

The men marched north away from the fort. "Hey, we better tell Isaac," I said. We climbed the ladder down from the mill loft and ran into the house to tell Isaac. He came back with us and climbed up into the mill loft. We watched while the men marched out of sight.

There was nothing to do but wait some more. There was quite a lot of firing in the distance now.

Sometimes it got louder and sometimes it died out altogether. I was scared. I wondered if Father was in
the fighting. Mostly Joe Mountain and I stayed in
the mill loft, watching to see if anyone was coming.
Every once in a while one of us would go down and
kind of stretch and walk around. Mother and Annie
stayed in the house, just moving restlessly around.
Isaac kept moving, too, first going up into the high
meadow to watch, and then down to the house, and
then the mill and back around again. He carried his
musket with him, and powder and shot.

The day went along. It got to be after supper
time and the shadows started to get longer. And just
about then, without any warning, we began to hear
a terrific noise of firing in the woods somewhere right
close to the mill.

"Do you see anybody, Joe?"

"I think it's coming from the woods," he shouted.

"We better tell Isaac." We dashed for the ladder
and climbed down out of the mill loft. As we hit the
floor I saw Isaac through the door, rushing out of the
house toward us, sort of dragging Annie along.
Mother was running behind them. They charged
across the mill yard, into the mill, and slammed the
door shut.

We were pretty scared. "Let's get into the woods,"
Annie said.

"Some of them are coming out of the woods," Isaac said. "They seem to be scattered all over the place." We went to the mill windows. There was a light haze of blue gunpowder smoke drifted in the air about a half mile away in the woods, up above the high meadow. Then a man suddenly appeared out of the woods on the other side of the creek. He was holding his arm, and there was blood all over his shirt. He stood at the side of the creek, trying to figure out how to get across.

"What happened?" Isaac shouted. The man glanced up at the mill, but he didn't answer. Then he decided he couldn't swim the creek with his wounded arm. He turned and ran along the bank toward the woods, until he was out of sight. Then another man popped out of the woods. He had no gun. He just dove into the creek, swam across, and began running toward Wilkes-Barre. Then came another, and another, all like the first, running and looking over their shoulders. Some of them dived into the creek, swam across, and then ran on down the road toward Wilkes-Barre. Others of them dashed into the woods.

"Those are Connecticut men," Mother said.

"What happened?" Isaac shouted. But they didn't stop. More men came, and more. Some were limping or hobbling along. Some were being sort of dragged

along with their arms over the shoulders of two
others, and one was being carried piggyback by another one. "What happened?" Isaac shouted.

But nobody answered. They just ran on. "God
damn," Isaac said. "It must have been a massacre."

"What did you expect?" Mother said bitterly.
"Outnumbered three to one and most of them Indians."

"Annie," Isaac shouted, "take the boys down into
the cellar. Now. Fast."

Annie's face was dead white. "The cellar," Isaac
shouted. He jerked open the trap door. "Find a place
to hide. Joe, go down first and help Annie down."
Joe climbed down the ladder and then Annie, and
then I went. It was dark and cool there. "No noise,
no lights," Isaac said. He slammed the hatch shut
and we were in the dark, with the smell of wet earth
and wet stone and flour all around us. The mill shaft
ran through a hole in the stone wall from the mill
wheel outside, and a little light came in through the
shaft hole—a thin trickle which showed up the shaft
and the shadowy fingers of the wooden gear cogs.

"Where shall we hide?" I whispered.

"Behind those barrels against the wall," Annie
said. "If we push the barrels out a little there'll be
room for us." Joe and I began pushing and heaving
at the barrels. Some of them were empty and pretty

light, but the ones full of cider and potatoes were pretty heavy, and it took both of us to shove them forward from the wall. We hurried; outside we could hear shouting and the sounds of guns exploding nearby. Scared as we were, it took us only a couple of minutes to get four or five barrels shoved out, making a little space behind them against the wall. We helped Annie climb over the barrels into the hiding place, and then we climbed in with her, and huddled down in the cold dark, me on one side of Annie and Joe on the other. Our bodies were pressed close to each other and I was holding Annie's hand. "We'll protect you, Annie," Joe Mountain said.

"Quiet, quiet," she said.

We sat in the dark, listening. We could hear the vague sounds of running and shouting, but they were sort of muffled by the stone walls of the cellar. Every once in a while a gun would go off—a big crashing explosion. Oh, I was scared, just scared to death nearly. So we waited; the shouting and banging went on and on.

And then suddenly there was an enormous crash from directly over us, and we knew that Isaac had fired his musket. "They're coming into the mill," Annie whispered. There was the sound of wood splintered and a confused hollering and shouting and then another great bang as Isaac's rifle went off again. And finally a loud long squeal like a wagon brake against the shoe and we knew that up there in the mill they were killing Isaac and Mother.

After that it was all sort of confused. There was a lot of trampling around and shouting for awhile. It seemed to go on and on.

Then suddenly the hatch door popped open, dropping a square of light down onto the dirt cellar floor. We could see feet in moccasins and parts of naked legs, and the barrel of a gun pointing down. There was talk and more shouting; and finally the hatch door banged shut and then a lot of footsteps and banging around and suddenly it was quiet up there in the mill. Outside there were running steps and shouting, and shooting in the distance. That seemed to go on a long, long time, too. But then finally everything was quiet and there was no sound but the rushing of the creek past the mill wheel.

"We should go up and help them," Joe Mountain said.

Annie shivered. "No," she said. "They're dead."

We wanted to cry but we were scared of making noise. So we sat in the dark and waited. The light coming in the mill shaft hole gradually went out and the tree frogs started to peep. I was cramped and chilly and scared to move. We just sat there and gradually I drifted off to sleep.

When I woke up Annie was jerking around, trying to stand up, and upstairs in the mill somebody was making a long, long cry, the kind of sound a crazy man makes. Then it stopped and the next minute the same voice, all harsh and twisted, shouted out, "Annie, Annie."

"Father," Annie shrieked. She struggled to her feet and so did Joe and I. I climbed over the barrels and just as I did the hatch door opened and there was Father, crouched down by the hatch, looking down into the darkness. "Is Ben there?"

"I'm here, Father," I said. "Annie and Joe are here."

"Oh, thank God, thank God." I helped Annie over the barrels and then I climbed up the ladder.

Father was still crouched by the hatchway as I popped up. "Don't come up here yet, Ben," he said. But it was too late. Isaac was lying by the mill door, on his face, and Mother was lying sort of on top of him, on her back, her eyes wide open and staring up at the roof. Both of them were scalped.

That afternoon Annie's baby was born. She named him Isaac, but she always called him Little Isaac, because she could never forget the other one.

4

*O*ut of the four hundred Connecticut men who'd gone out from Forty Fort that afternoon, all but sixty were dead by nightfall. It wasn't the British who'd caused most of the trouble, but the Indians. They'd taken two hundred and twenty-seven scalps, and maybe more. Father had been lucky. Being as they were outnumbered, the Connecticut men had been driven back until finally they were just fleeing. Father managed to get into the Susquehanna and hid there under the shade of some willow branches that hung over the water. Once a couple of Indians went by him so close he could have reached out and touched them; but they didn't see him, and after dark he worked his way up into the woods where he hid during the rest of the night.

After our army got defeated, the British and the rest just went up and down the valley for a couple of days, destroying things. They burned around a thousand houses—most of the farms in the valley. The Indians tortured a lot of people, and so did the Pennamites. Oh, there were terrible stories of people killing their friends, or even their own brothers who happened to be on the Pennamite side. I think the trouble was that the Indians and the Pennamites went sort of crazy. I asked Father about it. He said, "When homes and families are at stake, people do things to each other that's hard to believe."

But in the end, it hadn't done the Pennamites or anybody any good. The British couldn't stay there because there were some American troops on the way; so they just marched out of the valley, the whole lot of them, and the Connecticut people buried the dead and rebuilt the houses, and we went on with the mill business just as before—except that we were a different kind of family now, with Little Isaac instead of Big Isaac, and no mother.

Of course, right then was when Annie started talking about going back to Connecticut. She had no use for the Wyoming Valley anymore.

"I don't care how beautiful it is here, it isn't beautiful to me."

"We can't go back, Annie," Father said. "The soil's thin and stony back there, and there are too many people for the amount of land. We couldn't make a living."

"I don't care if there are too many people back home. There aren't enough out here. The soil here is bad too, it's full of my husband's blood."

"What would we do for a living, Annie?"

"We could live with Uncle John and work on the farm."

"Never," my father said. "I won't spend my life doing day labor for another man, even my brother. I don't want to live half a man. You have nothing to show at the end but your gray hairs and your stooped back."

I knew how Annie felt all right. For a long time it was hard for me to walk across the place on the mill floor where Isaac and Mother had been scalped. We washed up the blood, finally, but there was a spot there for weeks until eventually it got rubbed away by people's feet. Or I'd go into the house and there'd be a mug that had been Mother's favorite; and, of course, at the end of the summer we were eating the turnips and cabbages that she'd planted. It was hard to get away from thinking about her: she was just sort of everywhere.

But on the other side, I knew how Father felt, too. If we went back to Connecticut he'd have to work for Uncle John and so would I. And unless I was lucky in some way, I'd have to go on working for him all my life, Father said. I could never get married and have my own family, because there would be no way to support them, unless I hired out for wages. Father always said money wages are quicksilver, you have to spend them to live on, and to earn them you put your life into building up someone else's property and end up building nothing for yourself. I wouldn't be any better off than Joe Mountain.

So it was a hard thing to decide, but luckily, I didn't have to decide it. Father made the decisions, and he was bound and determined to stay in the Wyoming Valley.

"Even if we all get killed," Annie said.

Father shook his head. "How can you say that, Annie? If I'd known they were going to get killed I'd never have come out here. There was no way to know that."

And so time passed. At first I tried not to think about Mother. Then gradually my memory of the fighting faded out in my mind, and then I could think about her sometimes without getting all sick over it. I guess it was the scalping that bothered me the most. It doesn't have to kill you to be scalped. There was a soldier up at the fort who was scalped in

the French and Indian War and there wasn't anything wrong with him except that he had a big scar
just above his forehead. He used to say he didn't feel
a thing when it happened, he just lay still and pre-
tended to be dead. The other soldiers said he was
dead all right—dead drunk. So I didn't know
whether Mother felt anything when she was scalped
or whether she was dead already, or what; and after
awhile I stopped thinking about that part of it.

I wanted to talk to Father about her sometimes
but I couldn't. Once, about a year after she was
killed, we had pulled the millstone up, Father, Joe
Mountain and me, and we were dressing it with
chisels to sharpen the grooves. And I mentioned that
it was Mother's birthday. Father started to say something and then suddenly he began to cry. He walked
over to the window and put his big hand over his
face so that Joe and I wouldn't see the tears, but you
can't hold tears with your hands and they dripped
out between his fingers. So after that I never mentioned her to him anymore. But sometimes, when I
was alone out in the woodlot or bringing the oxen
up to the high meadow, I'd talk to Mother, not
aloud, but in my head. I'd tell her about Father
punishing me for something Joe Mountain did, or
about being sad for no reason I could think of, the
way I got sometimes. And then maybe I'd ask her if

she was scared when the Indians broke into the mill, and did she feel it when she was scalped. But naturally Mother never answered any of my questions. I figured she was in Heaven all right, but I wasn't sure if people in Heaven really could hear people on earth talk. Mr. Johnson, our minister, said that they could, but I didn't believe it. I guessed God could hear you, even though it was hard for me to figure out how he could understand thousands of people all talking at once. But that was all right. He works in mysterious ways His wonders to perform. But I wasn't so sure Mother could hear me. I mean why would she be listening to me instead of Father or Annie or Little Isaac? Or even Joe Mountain? You would think that maybe she wouldn't bother with Joe Mountain so much, being as he was a nigger, but if you want to know the truth, she'd raised him up, too, and he wasn't any different from me, even if he wasn't white. I mean being a nigger or an Indian was supposed to make you different, but I knew it wasn't so. So why wouldn't Mother be listening to him, too, sometimes? I figure that she would, if she could hear us.

Actually for us it worked out pretty well in one way. A lot of the farmers around had these small mills of their own. I mean maybe they might have a couple of thirty-inch millstones they could run with a small waterwheel, or even turn by hand. And they'd use the stone to grind their own corn and rye and maybe grind for a few neighbors, too. But in the massacre, some of the millstones got cracked and broken from the heat when the farmhouses were burned. Some other ones, well, the farmer figured it wasn't worth the trouble to rebuild his little water-wheel and the shafts and cog wheels that went with it. And then, of course, a lot of farmers had died, and their widows weren't able to run the little mills, even if they had them. It was easier to bring the grain in to our mill and pay us. They gave us three quarts of Indian corn for each bushel we ground, two quarts per bushel of wheat and rye, and one quart for a bushel of malt.

But there was another reason why a lot of these little mills stopped working. That had to do with the creeks drying up. When the settlers first came out to the valley there were hundreds of streams and creeks running through the woods. Because there was forest everywhere, the water soaked into the ground and went into the streams bit by bit. Then there were the beaver dams—great huge things sometimes scores of yards long. Of course, the beaver dams slowed the streams and creeks down. Between every-thing, the water just kind of meandered along. But after we settlers cut off the trees to make farms, the rain water would shoot right into the creeks instead of soaking into the ground. And when the beavers were killed off, the dams fell apart, and the streams speeded up. So what would happen was that after a rain, or in the spring when the snow was melting, the streams would go rushing along like mad, chewing up the banks and maybe even flooding over the sides. Then come the hot weather in July and August they'd dry up to a trickle. Some of them even dried up for good. So in the end, a lot of the farmers didn't have reliable streams anymore, and they couldn't run their little mills. It was just what had happened in Windham. You'd have thought grown men would have learned.

Naturally Father was very strong on keeping people from cutting too close to Mill Creek. If it didn't run steady our mill wouldn't be worth anything at all. We had rules in the valley about cutting along the creeks and rivers, especially the Susquehanna, but most of the land along the river belonged to somebody, and sometimes they would cut off the trees anyway, even if there were rules.

The next few years were pretty peaceful, and we ground our meal and gradually, when we had spare time, improved the mill. Mill Creek is just about twenty yards wide and about five feet deep. We had built a dam across it. I say we built it, but actually it was Father and Big Isaac who'd done most of the work. Me and Joe Mountain were too little to help much, but we helped some. The dam was just a row of big rocks heaped up in a line across the creek. To put them there Father loaded them on a raft. There was a rope tied to the raft and Joe Mountain and I pulled the raft out into the right place in the creek and then Father dropped the rocks off. Then, when there was a pretty good line of rocks across the creek, Father walked out on it and stuck boards down next to them, on the upstream side. We were always having to put in new boards, but gradually, as stuff washed down the river and got stuck in the rocks, it got to be a pretty good dam. Of course it leaked some in the cracks between the boards, but it held pretty well and made a millpond behind it about twenty yards wide.

The mill was alongside the millpond, just a little way up from the dam. It wasn't right on the pond, but back about fifteen feet. Father and Big Isaac had dug a kind of a channel which ran out of the millpond, then alongside it for fifty feet, and then back into Mill Creek below the dam. The channel was lined with stones so that the banks wouldn't wash out. It was about five feet wide. The mill wheel was in the channel and the mill right next to it. The mill wheel was about twelve feet tall. The water ran along the channel under the mill wheel and turned it around. The cellar of the mill was made of stone, because the water would have rotted it if it had been made of wood. The shaft from the mill wheel ran through the stone side of the cellar. Inside there were wooden gears attached to it, and these turned another shaft which ran straight up into the next floor. Up there, which was the ground floor, there were two millstones. The nether stone—the bottom one—sat on the floor. The shaft coming up from downstairs went straight through a hole in the middle of the nether stone. The upper stone was on top of the nether stone, but it didn't rest on it. Instead, it was fastened to the shaft with some metal parts which held it off the nether stone just a tiny bit—about the thickness of an oak leaf. The stones had kind of grooves in them, with sharp edges—at least as sharp an edge as you could get in stone. The grain—mostly corn or wheat or rye—poured down from the floor above into a hopper and then into a hole in the upper stone. As the stones moved around, the grain sort of spread about, and was ground up to flour. You'd be surprised at how powerful a thing like a waterwheel is. That upper stone weighed almost a ton, and yet it went around over a hundred times a minute. I know, because I counted it plenty of times. Of course those groove edges kept getting dull, and every couple of weeks or so we had to pull the upper stone off with a pulley and sharpen the grooves with chisels, which was pretty boring work.

Our house was just a log house, with a big chimney at one end. There was a loft over about two-thirds of it where Annie and Little Isaac slept. Father slept downstairs, and me and Joe Mountain slept in a sort of little shed we built up against the back of the house, where the chimney was. It's pretty nice and cozy sleeping right close to the chimney, because it stays warm all night. We didn't have much furniture: just a big table and benches in the middle of the room where we ate, and some chests for storing things, and over the fireplace, some cupboards for food. It wasn't very fancy—not as fancy as Uncle John's house back in Connecticut, where he had regular chairs, and glass in the windows instead of oiled paper, and china dishes instead of wooden ones, but I didn't mind about it not being fancy. I mean the woods were so pretty and in the hot weather we could swim in the millpond. Or on Sunday, when we didn't have to work, we could just lie on the bank of the creek and watch the fish playing around in the shallows. They were lovely fish—trout and bass and such, and good eating and easy to catch. As a matter of fact, one of the things I liked best about living in the valley was missing Sunday meeting. Mr. Johnson preached down at the fort in the village sometimes, but not too often. The other Sundays it was just Father or Annie reading from the Bible and they would take hardly any time for it.

So for the next few years after the massacre, that's the way we lived. Father had all sorts of plans. "We can't sit still," he would say. "A man can build something for himself out here if he's willing to work." Wilkes-Barre was going to expand, he figured. In time we'd have extra flour to sell. And when Father got some money together he figured he'd start a sawmill on the other side of the millpond; and then after that he wanted to get some more land of his own, so he could raise his own grain to grind and sell.

That was one thing that was great about being out in the Wyoming Valley—there was plenty of land for everybody. Land was riches. If we'd stayed back in Windham and lived on Uncle John's farm there'd have been just ninety acres for both families, and no way to get any more. But here on the frontier there were thousands of acres of land and hardly any people. It was like picking gold pieces off the trees. Everybody had a chance to become a lord or a squire or something. Having a lot of land meant you were able to be your own man, and your sons and grandsons, too. That's why Father had this saying, "It's better to be a bird in the wilderness than a lamb in the barn."

Oh, I loved hearing Father talk about all these

plans. Partly I just liked the idea of building things, of making things better. Partly it was the idea that when I grew up it'd be mine—mine and Little Isaac's, but mine mainly because I was the son and Little Isaac was only the grandson. And then maybe, if there was enough money, Father said he might send me to the academy back in Windham so I could learn to survey and keep accounts.

So the years went by. Joe Mountain and I grew bigger and older. And then in 1781 George Washington won at Yorktown and soon the Revolutionary War would be over. Joe and I were twelve. And it looked as if finally we were going to have peace. But the Pennamites hadn't forgotten. Once they asked the Congress to kick us out of the Wyoming Valley and give it to them. With the war over, the Congress had time to think about it. In November, 1782, they set up a court in Trenton, New Jersey, to consider the whole thing. I asked Father what he thought would happen. He shrugged. "I don't see how they can take our homes away from us. Even if they think we ought to be under Pennsylvania jurisdiction instead of Connecticut, they won't tear this settlement to pieces. It just wouldn't make sense after all the work we've put into it."

But that isn't the way it came out. On December 31st, 1782, the court ruled that the Wyoming Valley didn't belong to Connecticut; it was part of Pennsylvania. But they didn't say who owned the farms and houses and fields we'd taken out of the wilderness. And that spring two companies of Pennsylvania Rangers marched into the Wyoming Valley and took over Forty Fort.

We went into Wilkes-Barre to watch them march through town to the ferry to take them over to the fort. It was raining a spring rain. We stood in the doorway of a barn and watched them move slowly onto the ferry, all hunched up against the rain.

"Trouble," Father said.

"Why?" I asked.

Father spit out into the rain. "I don't reckon it's over for us yet."

"You mean there's going to be more fighting?" Joe Mountain asked.

Father stared out at the men on the ferry. "Maybe," he said. "I don't figure anybody here's going to give up their farms without a fight. Not after everything we've been through."

"Will you fight, Father?"

"I guess so," he said. "They killed your mother."

"That was the Indians," I said.

He didn't say anything.

"But how are they going to take the land?" I asked. "It's ours."

"That's not their view of it," he said, looking sour. "There's a Pennsylvania commission coming in to decide the claims. You can just figure how they're going to decide it." He spit out into the rain again. "They'll take everything all legal, and then they'll use the Rangers to run us out of our own houses for trespassing."

"They can't do that," Joe Mountain said.

"They can if they want to," Father said.

"We'll fight 'em," Joe said.

Father didn't answer.

I didn't believe it. "You mean they'll take our mill?"

"Maybe. There's probably been some land speculator back in Philadelphia or someplace who's had a claim on our land for years. Now he'll just come forward, show the commission his papers and they'll give it to him. After that it's just a question of running us off."

"But maybe you can convince him."

"The speculator? Oh, they won't all come out here. They're sending out only one as an agent to represent all the others. Alexander Patterson. He'll do the dirty work for all of them." He spit once more, then jerked his head toward home. "Come on, let's go back to the mill. I can't stand watching this."

We trotted back to the mill through the rain. Annie met us at the door. "Well?"

Father shrugged. "Pennsylvania Rangers."

She didn't say anything.

"Now, Annie, I don't—"

"Father, let's go back to Connecticut."

He didn't answer.

"Father, did you hear me?"

"I heard you, Annie."

"There's going to be fighting, Father. I don't want any part of that. We're going back."

He went on staring at the line of troops on the opposite bank. He didn't want to look at her. "Zebulon Butler's going down to Congress to talk to some people."

"Talk? What good will that do? I heard they already gave the land back to the Pennamites. Somebody in the village said it was already theirs."

He went on looking out through the rain. "Maybe," he said. "The court in Trenton adjudged it to the Pennamites. But Butler is trying to get Congress to reverse the decision, or at least let us keep our land even if it is in Pennsylvania."

"And if they don't?"

"If they don't, they don't."

"And then you'll fight. Isn't that right, Father? Look at me, Father. You'll fight. Isn't that right? Look at me and say so."

He turned to look at her. "I don't know, Annie," he said softly. "I don't know what we'll do."

"Is it worth getting some of us killed, Father?"

"You just leave this to me, Annie."

"Oh no, I won't. If there's fighting, I'm going back." She grabbed Little Isaac by the hand and dragged him out of the mill through the rain toward the house.

"She's pretty sore," Joe Mountain said.

Father shrugged. "She's worried about her child, that's natural. But what does she want me to do? I didn't ask the Pennamites to come back. I bought this piece out here in good faith, and paid for some of it with hard cash and some of it with hard work." He wasn't talking to us, really, just sort of talking to himself and staring out into the rain falling into the Susquehanna. "I worked sunup till sundown and more for seven years now and I've got something here. I have nothing to go back to in Connecticut." He turned around and looked at us. "You understand that, boys. There's nothing for us to go back to there except working Uncle John's farm for him. You wouldn't like that very much, would you, Ben?"

"I guess not," I said. "How come Uncle John got all the land?"

"That's the way your grandfather divided it. I got the mill, John got the land. When we came out here I sold John the old mill and the dry riverbed. It wasn't worth much, but it was enough to get us started here. I can't very well ask him to give it back to me, can I?" He looked back out at the rain again. "No, we're staying. Otherwise we might just as well turn ourselves into nigger slaves."

I didn't say anything. I didn't look at Joe Mountain, either.

5

week later a farmer named Simon Stone came to the mill with his wagon to pick up his grain. He had a bad arm—he had got shot in the shoulder during the 1778 massacre and he couldn't move his arm around very much, it just sort of hung there, although he could use his hand a little. Me and Joe Mountain helped him load the barrels onto his wagon. My father said, "Where are you going to store this, Simon?"

"In the loft," he said.

Father nodded. "You can't get it up there by yourself, Simon. The boys'll ride out with you and give you a hand."

"I appreciate that, Daniel."

We got into the cart and rode out to the farm. It was five miles out and we'd have to walk back, but we didn't mind that. Walking was better than working in the mill. The farm was a nice shingled house, with a log barn, all standing in the middle of the cornfield. We pulled through the field and as we came up to the house we saw three men on horseback in front of the house, talking to Mrs. Stone. Two of the men were Pennamite Rangers from the Fort.

Mr. Stone pulled the wagon up and stared at the men. "What is it?" he said.

Mrs. Stone turned to him. "They want the house, Simon. They say it isn't legally ours."

One of the men got down from his horse. Then he opened a saddlebag hanging over the horse's flanks. "You Stone?" he said.

"Yes."

"I have papers here showing that this house belongs to John Williamson of Philadelphia."

Mr. Stone sat in the wagon staring at the man. "Who are you?"

"I'm Alexander Patterson. I'm your new Justice of the Peace." He grinned and jerked his thumb at the two Rangers. "And these are my constables." He took some papers from the saddlebag and handed them up to Mr. Stone on the wagon. "Here's my authority," he said. Mr. Stone took the paper, read it

over carefully and then handed it back. Patterson
took it, put it back in the saddlebag, and took out
some more papers. "And this is an order for you to
vacate these premises forthwith. I may remind you
that as Justice of the Peace I am empowered to arrest
anybody who disobeys an order." He handed the
papers up to Mr. Stone, who took them and read
them carefully through. The Rangers sat on their
horses, looking bored. Mr. Stone went back to the
beginning of the papers and started to read them
again. Patterson began whistling. Then he stopped
and said, "This your nigger, Stone?"

"No," Mr. Stone said and went on reading.

Patterson looked at Joe. "Whose nigger are you,
boy?"

"He's ours, sir," I said.

Patterson looked at me. "Who are you, boy?"

"Benjamin Buck, sir."

"Buck? Who's your father?"

"Daniel Buck, sir."

"The miller?"

"Yes, sir."

"This is your father's nigger?"

"Yes, sir," I said.

"Is he registered?"

"I don't know, sir," I said.

"This isn't Connecticut territory anymore. It's

Pennsylvania land now. Under our laws if he wasn't registered under the Act of 1780, he isn't a slave anymore. He's free." He looked at Joe Mountain. "Do you understand that, boy?"

Joe Mountain didn't say anything. Patterson looked back at me. "Does he understand English?"

I didn't say anything.

"God damn it, when I ask you a question, you answer it, boy."

"I know how to talk," Joe Mountain said.

"Well, you answer when I speak to you, boy. Now do you understand that? If your master didn't register you, you're free. Understand?"

"Yes, sir," Joe said.

"What's your name?"

"Joe Mountain, sir."

Mr. Stone finished reading the papers. He handed them back to Patterson. "If we have to go, we have to go," he said.

"Simon—" Mrs. Stone said.

"Rebecca, we can't argue with guns," he said quietly. Then he turned to Patterson. "How much time have we got?"

Patterson put the papers back in his saddlebag and began buckling it up. "About as long as it'll take you to throw your goods in the wagon," he said.

Mr. Stone got down off the wagon, and walked

into his house. "Come on, Rebecca," he said.

And then about ten seconds later he was kneeling in the doorway. He was holding a Pennsylvania rifle at the throat with his good hand, and resting the barrel on his knee. It wasn't much of a way to shoot—the gun would blow out of his hands the minute he fired it. But he could get off one shot and kill one man, and Patterson and the Rangers knew it. "Get off my land, Patterson. I killed the man who ruined my arm and I don't mind killing another one."

Patterson stared at Mr. Stone. "Fire that rifle and these fellows would shoot you dead two seconds later."

"You'd go first, Patterson. They'd think mighty well of me around here for killing you. Now get off my land."

He stared at Patterson. Patterson stared back. Then he shrugged. "It doesn't much matter, Stone. We can always come back another day." He put his foot into the stirrup and swung up onto his horse.

"Come back if you want," Mr. Stone said. "I can kill you just as well tomorrow as today."

Patterson and the Rangers rode away. Mr. Stone stood up and leaned the rifle against the door jamb. His hands were trembling and his voice was hoarse. "Let's get that flour unloaded," he said.

We helped him stow the flour in the loft and then

we started for home. We walked along a mile or so, keeping an eye out for the Rangers. We figured they might double back to Stone's farm and we decided to hide if they came by again. "Probably they wouldn't do anything to us," I said. "I'd rather not take any chances, though."

"I guess so," Joe said. He was being pretty quiet. We walked on not saying anything for a while. I knew what he was thinking about, but I didn't want to bring it up. I didn't know why, I just didn't. But I didn't have to, because suddenly he blurted out, "Do you guess he was right about me being free?"

I didn't want to answer. I didn't know why.

"Do you guess?" Joe Mountain said.

"I don't know," I said. "Probably not."

He stopped walking and I stopped walking, too. "Why not? Why shouldn't he be right? Why shouldn't I be free?"

And suddenly I realized what I was feeling: I didn't want Joe Mountain to be free. I wanted things to stay just the way they were. I knew it was a bad thing to want, but I couldn't help myself. "I don't know," I said.

"Why shouldn't he be right? He said he was a Justice of the Peace, didn't he? He should know, shouldn't he? That means I'm free. I'm free standing here right now."

I felt pretty confused. "I don't know if that's right, Joe. He said you had to be registered or something."

"I'm going to find out," Joe said. "I'm sure as hell going to find out."

We walked on home. I couldn't understand why I felt the way I did, about not wanting Joe to be free. Oh sure, I wanted Joe to be my friend and go on the way we'd always gone, just like we were brothers and all that. I didn't want to suddenly start bossing him around or making him do my jobs for me. But still, I wanted to be the white man and him to be the nigger. That was the way it had always been.

Two days later Alexander Patterson and four Rangers caught Simon Stone in the middle of his cornfield without his gun. They beat him with their rifle butts and then they tied his hands behind his back and led him along on foot behind a horse back to Fort Wilkes-Barre, the fort that was right in the village. Father went down there to see if he could do something for him. He said that there was blood all over him, his shirt was ripped and there was a bad cut under his ribs. The next day his wife Rebecca walked into the mill with her little girl. She was carrying their clothes in a bundle on her back.

"They took everything," she told my father. "They took the wagon and the horse, everything.

They let me take out our clothes and the Bible, but that's all—no grain, no flour, no nothing."

"Is somebody in the house?" my father asked.

"Not yet," she said. "They're coming in today. Some Pennamite from Philadelphia. Williamson is his name. He doesn't have any family, just him alone. What does he want our farm for? He hasn't got anybody to feed but himself."

Father shook his head. "Better stay here with us for now," he said. "It's going to be bad times for everybody."

Father was right. The Pennsylvania government had sent in a commission, who were supposed to decide on land claims. But it was pretty much a joke. Patterson wasn't on the commission, but he was around the fort all the time, when the commissioners were deciding things. He was supposed to be an agent for a lot of Pennamites who were trying to claim our land. The way it worked was, Patterson would tell the commission that such-and-such a house belonged to some Pennamite. Well, the poor farmer would come down to the commission with his papers and deeds. He'd argue and plead as best he could. But then Patterson would show his papers and deeds. Well, then the farmer would say that he'd lived there for ten years, and had cleared the land and built the house and all that. And Patterson would answer that was too bad, but he shouldn't have been on the land in the first place. The three commissioners would sit there and listen to both sides and nod, and finally send everybody away so they could make their decision. And of course, being Pennsylvania men themselves, they always decided for Patterson and the Pennamites.

Patterson would go out to the farm with an eviction order and if the farmer didn't move off immediately Patterson would have the Rangers arrest him and jail him in the fort, and then he'd drive the wife and children out—just kick them out, with no place to go. It was pretty terrible being in jail, too. It was filthy in there and the food was awful and sometimes they beat the men with ramrods from their guns.

"It isn't fair," I told Father. We were eating dinner at the big table in the house. "It's just wrong."

"Patterson isn't a fair man," Father said. "He's cruel—that's his nature. He doesn't care what he does to anybody. Besides, he's one of the biggest of the speculators. He stands to make a lot of money if he can get us out. He wants to make things bad around here for everybody so we'll leave. He's trying to drive us off."

"I don't see why he has to do that," I said. "He's getting everybody evicted, anyway."

"He's in a hurry," Father said. "He knows that the

Congress could vote against the Pennamites any day."

"But they won't, Father," Annie said. "Patterson's going to win. We're going to have to go back to Connecticut sooner or later. Why do we have to suffer first?"

Father gave her a look. "Patterson is evil, but he isn't all-powerful."

Joe Mountain didn't say anything.

Mrs. Stone went back to Connecticut, and so did some of the others, especially women with children whose husbands had been arrested. We tried to take care of them—we let them sleep in the mill and we shared food with them, but as winter began to come along, there wasn't that much food to share. With so many farmers in jail at the fort, or gone back to Connecticut, there wasn't so much grain for us to grind. We began doing a lot of hunting, especially Joe Mountain. Joe Mountain boasted a lot about being brave and fighting everybody, but to be honest, he was a good hunter. He really loved going out into the woods with Father's gun, the Brown Bess we'd brought from Connecticut. I guess maybe walking around in the woods with a gun made him feel less like a slave. Anyway, lots of times he came home with rabbits and squirrels and sometimes with deer. He'd got a lot of the deer trails figured out. He knew where they were likely to be.

The funny thing was, Joe never mentioned again about being free. I would have thought he'd have asked Father about it, or maybe even tried to get some information about it from one of the officials up at the fort, although I guess he would have been pretty scared to do that. I mean boys, even big ones like us, wouldn't have the nerve to go making visits to important officials. Still, it seemed funny to me that he didn't bring it up with Father. I didn't think he'd forgotten about it; nobody just forgets about something like being free. But he didn't say anything to Father. I guess he was just scared to. He knew what Father was likely to say.

So summer came and went, and it just seemed as if we were waiting, just waiting for what we didn't know. Of course, the Connecticut leaders kept trying to get a new trial. Father was in on a lot of the meetings; being the miller, he was more important than an ordinary farmer and Colonel Butler sometimes stopped at the mill to talk to him about these things. But it was hard to get Congress to do anything, and in the meanwhile we got another bad blow. This happened in October. The Pennamites held elections for constables and other officers for the Wyoming Valley. But instead of holding them at Wilkes-Barre, they held them at a little tiny place called Pennsbury, which was ninety miles away from Wilkes-

Barre. It would have taken us at least two days to get up there and vote. But it didn't matter anyway because the Pennamites never told us they were going to have the election. They just had it. Actually, there were twenty-four Connecticut men living near Pennsbury, and they knew about the election. But the Pennamites threw out their votes. To vote you had to be living in Pennsylvania for a year. Of course, these men had been living there for years and years, but the Pennamites said no, that didn't count. They said that the Connecticut men had claimed that they had been living under Connecticut law all that time, so obviously they hadn't been living in Pennsylvania, they'd been living in Connecticut. It was a dirty trick, but there wasn't anything we could do about it. And so, after that, the Pennamites were bosses of the whole Wyoming Valley.

The cold weather began to come. The food situation got worse. One problem was the Pennamite Rangers. Another batch had come, making ninety all told. For food the troops just took people's livestock, grain, flour, milk, anything. "They call it requisitioning," my father said, "but it's just plain stealing."

"They pay for it, don't they?"

"Sure, with Continental paper money which isn't worth a tinker's damn."

Then one day Joe Mountain came in from hunting with a pair of rabbits over his shoulder. He dropped them on the floor of the mill. "Mr. Buck," he said, "somebody's been cutting trees along the Susquehanna."

My father jerked his head up. "What?"

"There are four or five fresh-cut stumps just up there toward Jerrold Short's house. They weren't there yesterday, so somebody's been out there at night, cutting."

"Damn," my father said. "Damn. We better go have a look."

We put on our jackets and went out into the cold, biting weather. It hadn't snowed yet, but there was a feeling in the air that the snow was about to come— cold and a little wetness and low, gray, lumpish clouds racing along overhead. We walked down the mill road to the Susquehanna and then turned left along the river in the direction of Wilkes-Barre village. The trees were thick along the bank—oaks and maples and everything else, just the way it had been when we'd first come out there. The bank sloped down to the water and there was a little path along the top, winding through the trees. Everybody who owned land along the Susquehanna, like us, had left the willows and maples uncut for about fifteen yards back from the river, to hold the bank. When the water ran high and fast in the spring floods it would wash the bank right out if it weren't full of the roots of trees and brush to hold it. Once the bank started to go, the water would cut deeper and deeper into your land.

We walked along the path a couple of hundred yards. Then Joe pointed. "See?" he said. At the edge of the path there were four stumps—two willows and two maples, their tops looking white in the gray light of the day.

We walked up to them and Father put his hand on one. "Still wet with sap," he said. "Weren't cut more than a few hours ago."

"They weren't cut yesterday when I came through just before supper," Joe said.

"Then they must have been cut last night or early this morning. You didn't see anybody, Joe?"

"No. I didn't hear anybody chopping, either."

My father kicked at the wood chips on the ground. Then he spit. "Let's go up to Jerrold Short's house. He might have heard it."

We turned and walked away from the riverbank through the forest line until we came to a clearing, where Short's dry, withered cornstalks stood in his field, tipping this way and that way like a lot of drunken men. Short's house was in the middle of his fields, like most of the farmhouses around. Running through the dirt in a straight line between us and the house was a line where the earth was scraped up and the cornstalks broken down. "Somebody's been dragging something through here," my father said. None of us had to say what it was. Father began to walk down the furrowed line and we followed him up to the house. There beside it lay four logs, their cut ends white and wet.

"Jerrold Short knows that's illegal," Father said. He looked good and mad and he started to go around to the front of the house; but just then we heard a door slam and Mr. Short came around the corner with a buck saw over his shoulder.

"Daniel," he said.

My father just pointed at the logs. Mr. Short shook his head. "I can't help it, Daniel," he said. "I've got to keep my family from freezing to death."

"Not with wood from the river bank," Father said. "That's against the law."

"That's Connecticut law," Mr. Short said. "That doesn't apply here anymore."

"Maybe it does and maybe it doesn't, Jerrold." Father spit onto the ground. "But if you cut along the river we won't have any bank by next summer."

"I can't help it, I have to cut somewhere."

"What about your woodlot?"

"That's cut."

"Cut? Already?"

"I've been cutting for the Rangers up at the fort.

They'll burn two hundred cords up there this winter and they're paying for logs. I can make four shillings a day that way. I can't pass up money like that, not the way things are now.''

''Damn it, Jerrold, what's the use of four shillings a day if the river's going to hell? You know what'll happen, it'll flood all over the banks in the spring. Your farm will be two feet under water every March.''

''I can't help it, Daniel, I've got to cut somewhere. By the time I get finished cutting for the fort it's after dark and if I don't cut close to home I'll never get the wood here.''

''What are you going to do about my mill? You kill the creeks around here, there won't be any mill to grind your flour with.''

''It won't matter, Daniel. There isn't going to be any corn if the Rangers keep taking it all anyway. I need money now, I can't worry about tomorrow.''

''I'm going to see about this, Jerrold. I can't stand by and let you ruin the riverbanks. I'm warning you, I'll bring the law down here.''

Mr. Short shook his head. ''That's Connecticut law. They won't enforce it. I'll tell you that right now, just to save yourself trouble.''

''We'll see,'' Father said. He turned and strode back across the field of withered corn and we followed him.

But Mr. Short was right and my father was wrong.

The next morning he went up to the fort to talk to the commissioners. He told us about it when he came back. "It's so stupid," he said. "Just because it was our law from before, when we were under Connecticut jurisdiction, they won't enforce it. I told them they'd have trouble sooner or later if they let everybody cut off the banks. We saw it happen in Windham. But they don't care. They're just speculators. They're not going to work the land, they're going to sell it to some poor soul back in Philadelphia or someplace and they don't care if the trees are gone and the streams dried up and soil washed into the river. The speculators will ruin the valley yet. The land ought to belong by right to the man who uses it, not to some fat sharper in a countinghouse back in Philadelphia."

"You mean they really don't care if the land washes out?" Annie said.

Father shrugged. "I don't know what they care about. All they said was that it wasn't my business to worry about it. They said that if I wanted to make trouble they'd show me what trouble was."

"So they'll ruin the land."

"All they're thinking about is making sure they've got wood enough for the winter. If they can't feed and house and heat those troops they'll all desert, and if the troops go, there's no way they can take the land away from us. So they'll cut wood wherever they have to."

"And so we're going to have another war," Annie said.

We looked at her. "I hope not, Annie."

"And maybe this time you'll get Ben killed, or me or Little Isaac."

"Annie, stop talking that way. Nobody wants a war."

"I won't stop talking. You may not want a war, but you're bound and determined to have one. There are the Rangers in the fort. What do you mean you won't have a war? You're headed for a war sure as anything, and you don't care which of us dies, just so you can hang onto the mill." She was so mad she was about to cry.

"That isn't true, Annie. We don't want a—"

"Yes, it is true. Yes, it is true," she shouted. "You don't care who you kill so long as you can keep your land."

"Annie," Father shouted. "Don't talk like that." But she was gone.

I just didn't know what to think about it. In a way, Annie was right. It would take a lot to get Father back to Connecticut. I don't mean that he'd want to get anybody killed. If it were between one of us getting killed and going back to Connecticut, why he'd go back. But he was willing to take a chance on it. I mean the way things were going, there might be another war. Nobody knew for sure. In fact, nobody around seemed to have much of an idea of what the answers were to it at all. Whether we got to keep the land or had to give it up didn't seem to be between us and the Pennamites. And now some Connecticut men like Mr. Short were siding with the Pennamites. It was always somebody somewhere else that seemed to have the say. I mean a court somewhere or Congress or some committee would take it all up and make a decision, and the first thing we'd know about it was when they'd tell us what they'd decided. Oh, I guess the Connecticut men in Congress were trying to fix it so we could keep the land—anyway Roger Sherman was, and he was the most important of the Connecticut men. At least that's what we heard out in the Wyoming Valley. But Father always said that there were a lot of considerations to it that we didn't understand. We just had to go along with the Connecticut leaders back East and hope for the best. So who could tell what was likely to happen—it seemed to me that the way things were going there was a pretty good chance we'd have another war. And then what would Father do? Would he go back, or would he take a chance on one of us being killed so he could save the mill.

After Annie ran out, I thought about this while I was working in the mill. And the thing that interested me most was what would I do if I were Father? Would I go back, or would I stay and take a chance on the war? The truth was, I didn't know how I felt, I didn't know what I would do. And so how could I blame Father if I didn't know which thing was right, either?

One thing that was wrong, though, was cutting off the bank. I could see that Father was right, it was just stupid. If we were going to get kicked out by the Pennamites pretty soon, making a few extra shillings wouldn't make much difference; but if we were going to stay, timbering off the rivers and creeks could make an awful lot of difference, because it would be killing them, at least the streams and smaller creeks. It made me mad just to think about it. Oh, it was their land, they could cut it off, but the river they were going to ruin wasn't just theirs. And it came to me that I ought to try to do something about it. I don't know why I thought it was up to me. I just did. And so at the end of the day, just at dusk, while there was still light enough to see by, I went out onto the riverbank path once more and began to walk upstream.

I didn't have any particular plan. I just thought I'd walk up a ways and see if Jerrold Short was cut-

ting or if anybody else was. I didn't know what I'd
do if they were, I just figured I'd find out. I came to
the stumps where Jerrold Short had cut. There were
still just four stumps, so I walked on winding
through the trees naked of leaves in the coming darkness, looking for signs of cutting. For a mile I didn't
see anymore. But then I came to a place where the
river looped. Where it bent across in front of me,
about a mile away, there were trees down and a light
patch in the forest. Two men were there with an ox;
it looked as if they were hitching logs to the ox to
drag them out of the woods.

It made me furious. I began to run along the path
as it followed the bend in the river. I didn't know
what I was going to do when I got there. I didn't
think about it. I just kept on running. At first the
men with the ox couldn't see me because I was hid-
den in the trees, but then I broke into the clearing
they had made by cutting. They heard the sound of
my feet and they stopped what they were doing to
watch me as I ran up. When I reached them I was
panting and hot. They were farmers from around—
I recognized them from seeing them at the mill, but
I didn't know their names.

"What is it, son?"

"Why are you cutting here?" I shouted. "Don't you
know it'll ruin the bank?"

They stared at me. "Who the hell are you?"

"It doesn't matter," I shouted. "If you cut the bank, that matters."

"What's your name, boy?"

I calmed down a little. "Ben Buck," I said. "And if you—"

"Daniel Buck's son?"

"Yes," I said. "You know you shouldn't cut here. Everybody knows that."

He put his hands on his hips. "Well, I'll tell you what, Buck. You just run on home. And when you get there, you can tell your father that if he doesn't keep his loudmouthed son from poking his nose into other people's business, somebody's liable to come down there and throw him into his own mill-pond."

I stood there staring at him. I wanted to hit him. "God damn, you—" He swung his hand around so fast I didn't even see it coming. It cracked against my nose and mouth and the next thing I knew I was lying on the ground, and they were driving the ox off across the clearing with the log dragging behind it. I sat up. My mouth was full of blood and I spit. My nose was bleeding, too. I walked to the bank, slid down it and knelt and let my whole face soak in the icy cold water. Then I swished some through my mouth. It stung, but it stopped the bleeding, and I climbed back on the bank and began to walk home. And the idea that went through my mind was that if I could get myself into a fight over a few trees getting cut down, was it surprising that men would have a war over a whole valley?

6

Seventeen-eighty-four was the hardest winter anyone could remember in the Wyoming Valley. It snowed again and again. Just when it started to melt and you figured the ground would soon be bare it would turn cold and snow again. It was cold work out in the mill, cold work everywhere, and the men continued to cut along the Susquehanna. Everyone was doing it. Toward the end of January we got one snowstorm that dropped four feet of snow on us. For almost a week it was impossible to get out of the mill and into Wilkes-Barre. We were trapped there, and food got short. In a deep snow like that hunting is almost impossible. You can hardly move along through the woods at all. Of course, a deer will flounder in the snow just like a man will, and if you come upon one he isn't hard to shoot, because he can't really run but has to sort of stagger along in jumps. But mostly the deer have sense enough to stay in the deep woods where it was a lot of trouble for us to get to, and the little animals could scamper on the top.

Oh, my, it was cold. It must have got way down below zero several times. In weather like that about all you can do is cut wood and keep the fires going. We hitched a sledge onto one of the oxen and pulled it up into the woodlot. After we'd gone up and back a couple of times it packed the snow nearly as hard as dirt, and we could get back and forth on it pretty easily. We spent half our time up there cutting wood. Our hands stayed pretty warm because we were using axes and saws, but standing there in the snow swinging an axe your feet didn't move very much and they got cold and numb, and it hurt like hell when they thawed out.

It was so cold the Susquehanna froze up solid. It was so hard that you could run wagons on the river. It was easier to travel around that way than it was on the roads. But then we had a thaw, like you sometimes get in January. The warm air came up quick on a south wind, and the ice on the river, instead of just melting back to water, broke up into great chunks, some of them big as millstones. The chunks of ice came down the streams and creeks into the Susquehanna, where there was plenty of ice already. When they hit a shallow place they'd stick, like a boat gone aground, and then other chunks would pile up behind the first one.

The worst part was that the big chunks wouldn't float over our dam. They stuck along the top, and then other chunks piled up behind them, kind of like a stone wall, so that the dam was raised up three feet with a wall of ice. Then suddenly the wind turned around again into the northwest. The cold came back as bad as before, freezing everything up again, so that the ice wall on top of our dam was solid as granite. The level of the water in the millpond began to rise. It got higher and higher, until it was ripping through the millrace in a torrent. If it got much higher it would come over the millpond banks and flood the mill. Besides, the torrent of water going through the millrace was very likely to smash up the mill wheel. We got axes, went out onto the ice wall on top of the dam, and cut notches in it for the water to flow out. It was pretty scary doing that, because the ice was so slippery and hard to climb around on. But we got some notches cut and the water burst out through them and the level of the millpond went down.

But the notches kept freezing up, and every couple of days Joe Mountain and I had to go out and cut away some ice. We had to cut ice off the mill wheel, too. The water in the millrace didn't freeze, because it was moving at a pretty good clip, but the spray it splashed up as it raced along would freeze on the boards and build up there until the entire wheel was covered with a couple of inches of ice, binding it fast to the stone side of the mill. It didn't matter much if it was frozen up; there wasn't any work grinding grain. But if we left the ice on eventually it would ruin the wheel. So Joe and I had to cut it clean of ice every morning. That was dangerous, too, because if you slipped off into the millrace you could be pulled under the wheel and drowned. It happened to a man Father knew back in Connecticut.

But there was an even worse worry. "It's a dangerous situation," my father said.

"Why?"

"If we get a slow thaw in the spring, a couple of warm days, then some cold days, then more warm, so that all that ice melts bit by bit, we'll be all right. But if we get a patch of good warm weather in March, she'll thaw fast and all that ice will go at once. It'll come down the river in big chunks and raise hell with anything it smashes into. It could make a mess of the dam."

It was bad times all right: a hard winter, the Pennamites giving everybody trouble, and not enough food. By the end of January a lot of people had decided to give up and go back to Connecticut. A whole bunch were moving up to New York State. Some others were prisoners in the fort, being held there on any flimsy excuse Patterson could think up. Some other ones decided to acknowledge the Pennamite claims and had bought their own land back. Of course, a lot of people, like us, hadn't got the money to do that even if they wanted to, especially the widows. It was bad times, and the question was whether Patterson would decide to take the mill, the way he'd taken the houses.

I talked about it one day with Joe Mountain when we were cutting wood out in the snowy mill yard. "Father thinks they might do it. He thinks they would have taken it already except that they haven't got another miller to replace him with. You've got to have a miller or nobody'll have any bread."

"I think the Pennamites are going to win," Joe Mountain said. "I think they're going to end up taking the mill and everything."

"Why do you think that?"

"Who's going to stop them?"

"Father said he thought the Pennsylvania government will take the Rangers out of here sooner or later. It costs a lot of money to keep them here. Father figures they'll get tired of paying for it."

"I hope they don't," Joe Mountain said.

It surprised me to hear him say that. "What do you mean?"

"I hope the Pennamites win," he said.

I set down my axe. "That isn't funny, Joe."

"I'm not trying to be funny. I hope the Pennamites win."

"You can't. How could you hope that?"

"If the Pennamites win I can be free," he said.

It was odd that that had never crossed my mind. I stopped and thought about it for a minute. Then I said, "I don't think you ought to trust what Patterson says."

"Why not? Would he lie about it?"

"He lies about everything else," I said.

"Well, I can find out, can't I? Somebody will know if I'm supposed to be free."

I didn't want to talk about it. I went back to chopping.

But Joe just stood there with his axe resting on a log. "I could ask the commissioners, Ben."

I stopped working again. "Well, I guess so. But I don't see what difference it makes."

"To be free?"

"Well, yes. I mean look, I'm free, and I'm just the same as you. I don't get anything more to eat or anything than you do, and Father's just as likely to beat me as he is you."

"Yes, but someday you'll grow up and be free."

"Well, that's just it, Joe. I mean suppose Father made you free, what difference would it make? You'd have to stay right here at the mill and go on working just the way you do now. It wouldn't change anything."

"I wouldn't have to stay here," Joe said. "I could travel around, and choose different kinds of work. You'll stay because you'll get the mill. But a slave can never own anything."

"Where would you go? Where would you sleep? What would you do for food?"

"There are lots of things I could do. I could go to Philadelphia and get a job. There's plenty of work there. Or maybe I'd be an Indian. Or I could be a miller. I know how to run a mill."

"But where would you get a mill? Where would you get your millstones and your irons and everything else? You'd just end up working for measly wages like Father says."

"I'd work for some miller in Philadelphia and save up my money and then I'd buy my millstones and come back out here in a few years and put up my own mill. There's going to be a need for more mills."

"And compete with us, I suppose."

"You won't be here. The Pennamites are going to kick you out."

"But if they don't?"

"I'll put up a mill in Pennsbury or someplace up the valley."

I could tell that he'd been thinking about it a lot. "It isn't as easy as you think to build a mill."

"It isn't as easy as you think being somebody's nigger, either," he said. "I'll tell you, Ben, I don't care what happens, I'm not going back to Connecticut with you—not if I can be free in Pennsylvania."

Well, I thought about it. Over the next few days I really thought about it a lot. It still bothered me, the idea of Joe being free, I'll admit that. I couldn't figure out why it should bother me, but it did. But on the other side of it, it bothered me that he wasn't free, either. A few times I tried to sort of close my eyes and hold my breath and see what it felt like to be a slave. Suppose it was me instead of him? Suppose all I had to look forward to all my life was working at the mill for Father, and then somebody else when Father died, and never get married and have a family because I had no way to support them? What would I feel about it then?

And then it occurred to me that if we went back to Connecticut, that's the way it was going to be. At least that's what Father said, and I figured he knew what he was talking about. If we went back I couldn't become a peddler or go into some business, because for that you need money to get started and we didn't have any money. I couldn't become a farmer because I didn't have any land and no way to get any. And I couldn't start a mill because there were too many mills in Connecticut. And even if there was work, it would be hard to get started again, because sure as anything Patterson wasn't going to let us take the millstones and irons and the rest of the things we needed away from Wilkes-Barre. The only other thing to do would be to go out into the wilderness somewhere, claim some land, and start farming it. But we'd been trying that, and where had it got us? No, if we left the Wyoming Valley I wouldn't have much choice but to work on Uncle John's farm. He'd be glad enough to have us. We wouldn't cost him anything except our food and clothing, and with us as extra hands he could probably buy some more land and farm that also, and make some money for himself from our work.

The more I thought about it, the more I could see that if we left the valley we'd end up about as bad off as any slave. If you didn't have land or money or something, nobody would want to marry you. You couldn't raise a family of your own and be boss of your own house, and try to build something for your children and your grandchildren, like we could if we stayed in the valley. If Father's plans worked out, in a couple of years we'd have a sawmill, and I figured he'd run that and I'd be boss of the mill we had now. And when Little Isaac grew up he'd run part of it, too. Then in a while, when we'd saved up some money from running the sawmill, he'd buy some land, and we'd grow our own grain, and sell that, too. There'd be a lot more settlers come out there; Wilkes-Barre would grow into a little town, and we'd be rich—well, I don't mean rich, but well-off—because we'd got out there first and worked hard. Oh, maybe it wouldn't work out this way exactly: there were a lot of things that could go wrong. But if we went back to Connecticut, we wouldn't have any choice. We'd be Uncle John's help for the rest of our lives.

So I sort of knew how Joe felt about being a slave. And I wondered what he would do if we had to go back to Connecticut. Lots of slaves ran away, and if they got into some free place, they could stay free. Or sometimes a nigger could figure out a way to make some money and save up and buy his freedom from his master. But to do that you had to have some way of making money, and Joe didn't have any. Running away was easier, and knowing Joe Mountain I figured he would probably try to run away sometime. But that was risky. If he got caught he could be in bad trouble.

Well, I thought about it. I thought about it at night when I went to bed and I thought about it when I was off working by myself somewhere. The thing was, I was supposed to be Joe's best friend. If he wanted to be free, it was up to me to help him. I could see that there was no way out of it, I'd have to say something to Father about it, whether I wanted to or not. If I was willing to get into a fight with somebody to save a tree, I ought to be willing to do something for my friend. There was one thing, though, that I wished I understood: why did it bother me to think of Joe Mountain being free?

Of course, I knew that Father wasn't going to be in favor of letting Joe go. I would have to think up some good arguments for it. So I thought about it for a day, but I couldn't come up with any arguments— not ones that Father would agree with, anyway. And I decided that I'd just have to bring it up, whether my arguments were good or not. So I waited until I got my chance to speak to him alone; and finally, a couple of days later he took me up to the fort to help him with a load of flour, and I saw my chance. It was a cold day, with a bitter wind, and we sat kind of hunched up on the wagon.

"Father," I said, "I've got to talk to you about Joe."

"Joe Mountain?"

"Yes," I said.

"All right, go ahead."

I took a deep breath. "You remember the day last fall when we were over at Mr. Stone's, and Patterson came along? You remember, Mr. Stone got his gun, and—"

"I remember."

"Well, Patterson said something funny to Joe Mountain. He told him that under Pennsylvania law, if we didn't register him before, he was free now."

"Patterson said he was free?"

"Well, I didn't exactly get it. It had something to do with being registered. I think the idea was that you had to register your niggers or they wouldn't be slaves anymore and could go free."

"I never heard of that law," Father said.

"Maybe it isn't true."

He shrugged. "Maybe, maybe not. We never paid much attention to Pennsylvania law out here—this was Connecticut territory."

"So you don't know if it's right?"

"No," he said. "Anyway, what difference would it make to Joe? What would he do if he were free?"

"Well, I don't know, Father, but he wants to be free."

My father turned on the wagon seat and took a look at me. "You've been talking to him about being free?"

"He brought it up a couple of times. Do you think it's funny for him to bring it up?"

"You shouldn't encourage him, Ben. I need him around here."

It surprised me that my father would say that. It sounded like he didn't have any feelings for Joe Mountain. "Father, why is it fair for me to be free and Joe Mountain to be a slave?"

"You're white. Joe's a nigger. That's plain enough."

"What difference does it make?"

"Niggers aren't the same as white people. They're not as smart as we are. They can't take care of themselves right. You set a nigger free, he's likely to starve to death. They're like children."

"I don't think Joe Mountain is so dumb," I said. "I don't think he's any different than me."

"Well, he is," Father snapped. "You don't think God gave him that black skin for nothing, do you?"

"Well, I—"

"I don't want to hear any more argument about it, Ben. I don't want you encouraging Joe Mountain in this line." He paused and got hold of his temper. "I like Joe Mountain and I've treated him almost like a son. I've treated him as good as I've treated you. He's a human being even if he is a nigger, and I would never treat him hard. But he's got his place and he's got to keep it." He stopped for a minute. "Anyway, Joe shouldn't trust Patterson. He's likely to give Joe some big story about being free, and then take him back to Philadelphia and sell him to some Virginian. He'd be a lot worse off on a plantation than he is now, living in our family. When you think about how most slaves live, he ought to be grateful for us."

I knew there wasn't any point in talking about it anymore, and I shut up. But the thing I couldn't get out of my head was, if we didn't want to be slaves to Uncle John, why would Joe Mountain want to be a slave to us?

The winter went on bad. February passed and it got to be March. The rivers were still frozen solid and those great chunks of ice were still stuck in the creeks and piled up along the dam. Joe and I spent a lot of time just keeping the mill wheel clear and notching the ice wall across the dam so the millpond wouldn't overflow into the mill. Oh, it was cold work; our fingers and toes would get numb and, of course, we'd be all wet and have to strip down in front of the fire and let our clothes dry out before we could get on with our chores.

My father was pretty worried about it, and every few days he'd walk back up Mill Creek and have a look at the situation. "It's bad up there," he said. "There are chunks of ice all the way back for a mile or more. If we get a fast thaw the whole business could break loose and come crashing down on us. It'll sure raise hell with the mill wheel if it does."

We were looking forward to spring all right. We were tired and cramped from being cold and wet all the time. We ached for a little warm sun. We looked forward to April. Especially Little Isaac, who was itchy from being inside so much. So, in the second week of March I was pretty pleased when I got up one morning and it was warm—above freezing for the first time since January. There were thick, heavy wet clouds everywhere.

"Rain or snow," Joe Mountain said as we ate breakfast in front of the fire.

"Rain," my father said. "We better keep a good watch out on that river. A lot of rain will break it up."

It began to rain early in the day and by afternoon it was coming down in torrents, great sheets of water slanting back and forth as the wind shifted around. Father and Joe and I sat in the mill, mending barrels, and watched through the windows the sheets of rain blowing back and forth. "It's nice to be warm for a change," Joe Mountain said.

My father shook his head. "Warm as hell. It must be pretty near fifty degrees. I don't like it warming up this fast. This rain is going to melt those rivers in no time." He paused. "I think maybe one of you boys better go upstream a ways and have a look."

"In the rain?" I said.

"It won't hurt you to get wet. You can go out naked and dry off when you get back."

I looked at Joe. "I'll flip you for it."

My father looked up from the barrel he was working on. "Joe can go."

"We can flip for it, Father."

"No, I want Joe to go."

I looked at Joe and then I looked away. He didn't get it. I guess he just thought that Father had some other job he wanted me to do. So he stripped off his clothes. "Where shall I go?"

"Go up Mill Creek a ways and then back to the Susquehanna and see what we've got, Joe."

He nodded and then he darted out into the rain, and I could see him through the window, his black body shining with the water and his long black hair sticking to the back of his neck. "Father, I wouldn't have minded going."

"No," he said, "I wanted Joe to go."

Half an hour later, Joe was back, standing wet and shivering in the mill, the water running off him in torrents. Father gave him some cotton sacking to dry off with, and he rubbed himself down, his teeth chattering. "It's beginning to break up. There's water running on top of the ice on Mill Creek, and some of those big chunks are beginning to float."

"What about the Susquehanna?"

"It's moving. It's full of ice and it's moving."

"I don't like it," my father said.

It rained all that day and when we woke up in the morning it was still pouring down in a flood. We kept going to the door to look at it during breakfast. "Is it going to flood us?" Little Isaac asked.

"No," Annie said. "Don't worry about it."

"I want to go see," he said.

"No," Annie said. "I don't want you going out there and getting soaked."

Mill Creek was running now, carrying chunks of ice down with it. They crashed into the dam. Some of them rose up and fell over the other side of the ice wall, and some of them just stuck there. The notches we'd cut got blocked up pretty quickly. The mill-pond was rising. By the middle of the afternoon it was only a few inches below the banks. Father sent Joe out again to have a look at the Susquehanna.

"It's Ben's turn to go," Joe said.

"I want you to go, Joe."

"But I went last time."

"I'll go," I said. "I want to go."

"No, I want Joe to go and I don't want any argument about it." He turned away. Joe stared at his back. Then he took off his clothes and went.

"Father, that isn't fair."

Father looked at me. "No," he said. "The other way wasn't fair. It wasn't fair of me to bring Joe up thinking he could live the same as a white man. He's got to learn, and the sooner he learns, the less it's going to hurt him later on." He looked me in the face. "He's property, Ben. I ground Colonel Dyer's corn for years and never got a penny—just a little three-year-old sambo. I fed him and clothed him, and your mother took care of him when he was sick for years before he was any use to us. He's an investment, Ben, like the millstones. Do you think it's fair for him to grow up thinking he's just the same as you, when pretty soon you're going to be his master?"

I couldn't say anything. I just looked down at the ground.

In the time it took Annie to cook up some johnnycake, Joe was back. He was pretty excited. "The Susquehanna is way up, pretty near to the top of the dock. It's full of ice just ramming along and it looks like it must be flooding upstream, because there's a lot of stuff coming down—a lot of wood and a barn door and some fence rails and I saw a drowned sheep."

"Bad," my father said. "Bad."

That was March 14th, and it went on raining, those great sheets of warm water filling the creeks and streams and breaking loose the ice; and then the whole lot—water, ice, logs—roaring down the Susquehanna. But what worried us most was the stuff coming down Mill Creek. A couple of times we went out into the rain with poles and tried to pry some of the ice off the top of the dam, so that the millpond would go down, but we couldn't do it. We thought about trying to crawl out onto the dam and chop the ice loose with axes, but Father wouldn't let us do it. "Too dangerous," he said. "If you slipped out there you'd be carried off and mashed to pudding by the floating ice."

By night time, however, the rain began to slacken off a little. "If the rain stops it won't flood," Joe Mountain said.

"I don't know," my father said. "There's an awful lot of water up in the hills still coming down."

"Will it come in the house if it floods us?" Little Isaac asked. Nobody answered him.

By the time we went to bed there was only a slight

drizzle, and when we got up in the morning the rain had stopped altogether. The skies were still cloudy, but a fresh wind was blowing and it looked as if it might clear off altogether soon. But when Joe and Father and I walked down to the Susquehanna, we knew we were in for trouble. The dock was gone— not just covered with water, but totally gone. And the water was over the bank. Normally the water ran five feet below the bank. It was a queer feeling to stand on top of the riverbank and have the water rushing by six inches from my toes.

There was a lot of stuff in the water, too. Most of it was logs and planks and boards, but there were other things: a chair and a couple of barrels and some drowned chickens and sheep, and a rowboat upside down, all rushing along on the river. "That's bad," Father said. "It's been flooding people out upstream, and that means we've still got high water to come." He pulled a small branch from a tree and stuck it into the muddy riverbank right at the water's edge. We watched; and five minutes later the water swept it away. "Rising fast," Father said. "They'll be damn sorry they logged off the riverbank now."

By noon it was well over the bank and creeping back up toward the mill. We went down and watched it. There wasn't anything else to do but watch. And we were standing there when there came around the bend a family in a rowboat—a man and a woman and a couple of kids. The man and the woman were side by side on the center seat, and they were pulling hard at the oars, trying to slide the boat across the racing current toward the shore. The water didn't want to let them go. If they cut across the current too sharply they'd be swamped, but when they tried to come toward shore at a smaller angle the current kept nudging them back into midstream. They were maybe a quarter of a mile upstream from where we stood, and they were coming fast. "Ben, quick," my father shouted. "Run up and get some rope." I turned and ran, and by the time I got back five minutes later the rowboat was only a couple of hundred yards away. But they had got the boat closer in to the bank, and they were still angling in.

I handed Father the rope. He coiled it up. "Swing in as close as you can," he hollered. "We have a rope." The people in the rowboat didn't answer, but continued to struggle with the oars, trying to move the boat across the heavy current. The boat was rocking and bouncing and plunging on the surface of the water, now only about a hundred feet from shore.

"Closer, closer," my father shouted. We could see them straining on the oars, white-faced, backs bent. The boat slammed on down the current, still edging closer in. They swept abreast of us. Father flung the rope. It arched out over the water, uncoiling, and fell across the rowboat. The man dropped his oar, grabbed the rope, and wrapped it swiftly around the seat. Father raced back away from the bank to the nearest tree, ran twice around it with the rope, and pulled it, snubbing the rope tight. The boat swept on by us, and then jerked to a halt as the rope snapped up out of the water, flinging a fine spray into the air. The boat swung around at the end of the rope and slid up to the bank. Joe and I ran over, grabbed the rope near the prow, and pulled the boat up onto the mud. The man helped the children out, and then his wife, and then got out himself. The children were crying. Together we pulled the boat up across the slippery mud onto land, ten feet from the water's edge.

"That won't do," the man said. "There's a flood tide still coming down. You're going to see a lot more water than this before nightfall."

7

We took them up to the mill, let them dry out in front of the fire, and gave them some hot soup. The man told us all about it. "There's water fifteen feet deep back there at Jacob's Plains. There's whole villages gone, twenty or thirty houses just wiped out—farms, livestock, barns, everything. There's more food in the river right now than in all the barns in the Wyoming Valley. Hell, there aren't hardly any barns left, anyway. Back at Swetland's there's water over the whole plain, back to the hills. The river's two miles wide there."

"How long do you figure before it'll get down here?" my father asked.

He shrugged. "Hard to tell. Nightfall, maybe. When she comes, she'll hit real fast. If I was you I'd be up in the hills long before dark."

"What are you going to do?"

"Give up and go back to Connecticut, I guess," the farmer said. "My house is gone, my barn's gone, my livestock's gone, my winter rye's under five feet of water."

"You're just going to let the Pennamites walk in and take over your land?"

"They can have it. Let them suffer for a while."

My father looked at Annie, and then he looked away again. Annie didn't say anything, but she kept her eyes on Father. "What'll you do back there?" he said.

The farmer shrugged. "I'll find something. It won't be like owning your own piece, but I'd rather that than see my kids drowned or scalped or locked up in the fort."

Father didn't say anything about that. They finished up their soup, and left to go back up into the hills and wait for the flood waters to roar through Wilkes-Barre. "It's coming," he said. "No doubt about that."

After they'd gone Father and me and Joe walked

down to the Susquehanna. The water had come up a good foot in the time we'd been gone. "Do you think it'll flood the mill, Father?"

"Hard to tell," he said. "If it gets high enough it'll start backing Mill Creek up. And if that ice on top of the dam lets loose all at once you'll have water all over the place." He shook his head. "Can't tell. I guess we'd better move whatever we can onto high ground."

So that's what we did. Annie and Little Isaac began packing our dishes and pots and our clothes into baskets and barrels and boxes, and Father and Joe and I carried the stuff up the hill in back of the house and a good half mile into the woods. We were pretty far above the Susquehanna there. It would take some flood for the water to get that high. We kept on working until it got too dark to see anymore. I never realized we had so much stuff. Besides the things we had in the house there were all our tools—saws, axes, shovels, awls, planes, hoes, rakes, and then of course all the special tools we used in the mill. Spread around the way it normally was, it didn't seem like much, but carrying it a half mile into the woods on your back it seemed like plenty.

But by nightfall we had most of what we could easily carry up there. We tied the chickens up in bags and took them up, and then we drove the oxen up there too, and staked them out under the trees. They didn't like it very much: it wasn't familiar to them, they liked being in the high meadow much better. Then we built a fire, and settled down for the night. The ground was still wet from the rain, but we cut some pine branches to make soft places to sit on. We cooked supper over the fire—just some johnnycake, but it was hot and good—and sat there waiting. It was pretty cold out, but we were warm close to the fire. There were other fires around us in the woods. Some of them were people like us, just up there to wait out the flood, but most of them were people from upriver who'd been wiped out by the flood and hadn't any homes to go to.

It was a clear night. There were plenty of stars out, and a bright moon, and you could see pretty well. "Will we be able to hear the flood when it comes, Father?"

"I don't know. I don't guess so, not over the noise of Mill Creek."

I was curious. So was Joe. He said, "Come on, Ben, let's walk down a ways and see if we can see it." We got up from the fire and walked back down the path until we got to where there was a clear patch ahead in the woods. Way in the distance was the Susquehanna, a broad band of silver. From the distance it didn't seem to be moving, but just lying still in the moonlight. "Let's go closer," Joe said.

"We better ask Father," I said.

"Let's just go," Joe said.

"No, we better ask Father," I said.

So we went back to the fire. "Father, we want to go down to the high meadow and watch the flood come."

He thought about it. "All right," he said. "It wouldn't hurt to know what's happening. But stay back of the house, up in the high meadow. Mill Creek can get over the banks pretty far up, and if it floods over up above you it'll sweep you down into the Susquehanna. As soon as something happens come on back up and let me know."

We left. We were excited and we jogged most of the way back down through the woods because we were afraid we'd miss something. It took us only about ten minutes to get to the rail fence at the top of the high meadow. We climbed over it and looked around. The Susquehanna was still a silver band, but from closer it was huge, more than twice as wide as it usually was. We could see it moving now, flooding along full of things, sort of carrying them on its back. It had reached up halfway to the mill—maybe two hundred yards beyond its banks. Mill Creek was running like hell, too—just boiling along down beside the high meadow, carrying along with it chunks of ice, and a lot of branches and logs, too. It roared down into the millpond, and then poured out through the notches we'd cut in the ice wall on top of the dam. The notches had been widened by the warm weather and the water rushing through, but there was more water coming down than they could take, and the level of the millpond was way up, really right to the banks. The noise was awful. We had to shout to hear ourselves. "If it goes any higher," Joe said, "it'll break out of the pond and run into the mill."

Down below, where Mill Creek ran into the Susquehanna, you would normally see some eddies where the two met. But now there was a great big sort of boiling pool, all churning around and around, heaving and splashing. A man who got caught in that had no hope—he'd go under in a second. It was pretty scary to watch, because as the Susquehanna crept up toward the mill, that boiling pool moved up, too. You could almost see it move. I mean you couldn't actually, but if you marked the spot where it was with your eyes and then looked away for a minute or so, when you looked back it would be closer.

"It's going to get the mill," Joe said.

"Maybe not," I said. It would be terrrible to lose the mill. "Maybe it's as high as it's coming now. Maybe it'll start going down."

"Naw," he said. "It's going to get the mill."

It was threatening from two directions. The Susquehanna could creep up from below until it washed into the mill; or the millpond could overflow and flood into the mill from above. We stood in the high meadow watching, and trying to make out the stuff racing along on the Susquehanna. In the moonlight it was hard to tell what it was. Every once in a while we could hear a cow bellow, and we wondered if it might be dashing along in the current trying to keep its head above water. We could see big shapes which we knew were houses and barns, and smaller shapes which could have been boats, or maybe sheds and chicken coops or barrels or trunks.

"Let's go down closer," Joe said.

"Father said to stay in the high meadow."

"I don't care, I'm going down."

"Me, too," I said. We started to run down through the high meadow. In a couple of minutes we came into the mill yard. It was all a swamp of mud, and we could see now that water had been leaking over the bank of the millpond and running down into the mill yard. But there was no water in the mill yet. "Joe, what'll we do if the mill goes? How will we live?"

He shrugged. "It's going to go, Ben. You better make up your mind to that."

"It can't go," I shouted. "What'll we do then?"

He shrugged, but didn't say anything.

"Listen, Joe, if we could pry some of that ice off the top of the dam the millpond would go down. We might save it."

"Hell, we can't do that. You couldn't move that ice with a team of oxen. There's tons of it."

"We can try."

"Well, I'm not afraid to try."

We went into the mill and I opened the hatch and started down into the cellar, to get a timber we could use for a kind of battering ram. It was pitch dark, but as soon as I got onto the ladder I knew there was water in the cellar. I eased down, sticking my foot to feel for the water. It was up two feet from the floor. "Hey, Joe, it's full of water down here."

"The water's so high in the millrace it's leaking in through the shaft hole," he said.

"I'll never find anything down here," I said. I climbed back up the ladder. "There's a wagon tongue in the woodshed," I said. We got it and carried it back to the end of the dam. There was a lot of water sloshing all over the place, cascading around the end of the dam. Just looking at the ice on the dam, my heart sank. I knew there wasn't any hope of knocking it loose.

"It won't work," Joe said.

"Let's try." We lifted the wagon tongue, me in the middle, Joe at the back end. "Heave," I said. We rammed it forward. It hit a chunk of ice and just slid away. "Once more," I shouted. We rammed it forward again, and the same thing happened.

"I told you it wouldn't work." We carried the wagon tongue back and put it in the woodshed. There wasn't anything more to do but pray that the water would start going down before it hit the mill. We walked back out of the mill yard and sat on the fence at the bottom end of the high meadow, to keep our feet out of the mud. We were both soaked, and cold, and beginning to shiver, but we didn't want to leave. We just sat there watching the Susquehanna roll along. By now it was about halfway up to the house, carrying with it that boiling pool where Mill Creek rushed into it. "It's still rising," Joe shouted.

I didn't say anything. All I could think was that if the mill went, we'd be finished. "Do you think it'll get the house, too?"

"I don't know," Joe said. "Maybe. But it's further back and maybe it'll be safe."

"We'll have to live in the woods if the house goes," I said.

"No, you won't. You'll go back to Connecticut," Joe said.

"What do you mean, *you?*"

He didn't say anything. We sat there watching. And then all of a sudden I felt something on my foot and I looked down. A broad torrent of water was rushing down under the bottom rail of the fence, lapping at my foot. I swiveled around. Behind us the bottom part of the high meadow wasn't a meadow any more, it was a lake. "Joe, look, the millpond is over its banks," I shouted.

He turned to look. "Let's get out of here," he shouted.

We jumped over the fence into what used to be the high meadow. Now it was a sheet of silver, rippling in the moonlight. The millpond had jumped its banks up where Mill Creek ran into it. Already it was a foot deep, and tugging strong at our legs, and it was rising fast. We slogged through it, but by the time we had got twenty feet from the fence it was above our knees. "It's strong," Joe shouted. It tugged so hard that we could only move one step at a time, first stepping forward with one leg, then planting that foot and swinging forward the other. It was like trying to walk into a wild wind. Each time I took a step I could feel the water cutting the ground away under my feet.

We pushed on. And then suddenly Joe's foot slipped on the slick, grassy bottom. He swung around, trying to get his balance, and the water knocked his legs out from under him. He disappeared into the water. Then I saw him, just a jumble of arms and legs flailing around in the water, rushing past me on the flood. I dove onto him. His knee smacked me in the mouth, but I got a grip on his shoulders and dug my feet into the ground. He turned over and kneeled up in water, then we sort of grabbed onto each other and stood up. By now the water was up to the middle of our thighs. Hanging onto each other, we pushed on, a step at a time. Under us the ground of the high meadow was rising. We began to come up out of the flood. As we climbed out of it, the walking was easier, and then finally we could run and sprinted out of the flood into the top part of the high meadow, flung ourselves onto the ground, panting and tired, and stared back down to where we had come from.

The water that had broken out of the millpond was racing in a great sheet through the mill yard, belting up against the back wall of the mill, and curling around both sides. We watched for a minute, and then the door burst open and the water began flooding through the mill and out the other side. You couldn't tell where the Susquehanna was anymore. Below the mill there was one huge boiling lake that stretched out everywhere as far as we could see. The water pouring out of the pond was cutting a wide path through the mill yard. The water level in the pond was going down, but that was because half of

Mill Creek was now pouring down the high meadow and into the mill instead of into the pond. With it were coming logs and branches and hunks of ice, slamming and banging against the back wall of the mill.

"It's going to go, Ben."

I didn't say anything, I just sat there watching. And then suddenly I realized that the mill was moving—sort of shaking, like a horse getting ready to turn loose.

"It's going," Joe Mountain shouted.

And then it went. First it sort of jolted off the stone walls of the cellar, and for a moment sat a little bit stuck on something. Then it seemed to bulge out. The rear wall splintered, and suddenly the whole mill was gone, racing down the flood toward the river. We saw it twisting and turning in the current. It fell over on its side, and then it was swept into the main body of the river and disappeared around a bend.

We sat there for I don't know how long in the moonlight, watching Mill Creek pour down over the place where the mill had been, feeling sort of numb and cold. Everywhere there was nothing but a big silvery lake, water as far as we could see into the dark, and out there more things than ever were moving on the surface. Most of the time it was hard to know what we were seeing: it was all just big black shapes. But we went on sitting there watching things rip along and arguing about whether it was a barn roof, or a big chunk of ice, or an upside down boat, or what. And along with the stuff floating down the river there were the noises—the rushing of the Mill Creek, the pounding of ice chunks against the dam. But mostly what got us was the livestock—cows and oxen bellowing and sheep squealing and horses neighing, and it gave us a creepy feeling because we knew that most of them were in the river and would probably drown. Once, all of a sudden, we heard a cock crow. We knew it had to be somewhere near us, because with the noise of Mill Pond we couldn't have heard it at any distance. We stood up; but we couldn't see it anywhere.

"We ought to go tell Father," I said finally.

"It doesn't make any difference now," Joe said. "There isn't anything he can do."

"Yes, but he'll get worried about us."

"Let's stay a little more, I've never seen a flood before."

"All right," I said.

So we stayed. Once we heard human voices, a long, long shout, as if somebody was trying to find somebody else. "He must be in a boat," Joe Mountain said.

"Maybe he's hanging onto part of a roof," I said.

"Do you think he'll drown?"

"Well, he might," I said. "If he could get over to shore he'd be all right."

"I guess there aren't hardly any shores anymore," Joe said. "It wouldn't be easy to get to shore. If it was me, I'd try to swim for it."

"Oh, you couldn't do that, Joe, not in that current. Nobody could swim in that current."

"I could. I'd try, anyway. What's the use of just hanging onto your roof or your boat or something? You're going to drown anyway, you might as well try to swim for it."

"Well, maybe you'd be better off hanging onto the boat," I said. "I mean maybe the river will go down pretty soon and if you just stick it out you'll hit onto a piece of land somewhere and be safe."

"Hell, that river isn't going to go down for days," Joe said. "Forty days and forty nights it took Noah's Ark."

"But then they bumped into land and were safe and the sun came out. They lasted it out forty days and forty nights and they were safe."

"But people here don't have any ark," Joe said. "They're just tearing along on the roofs of their barns and such. It isn't the same thing."

"I think we better go back and tell Father."

"Just a minute longer," he said.

"We should go back now," I said.

"You go back, then."

"You have to come back, too, Joe."

He didn't say anything for a minute. Then he said, "You go back, Ben. I'll come along in a minute."

"We should have gone back before. Father said to come back if something happened."

"We don't have to go back. He said somebody should come back and tell him."

"Then why should I go?" I said. "Why not you?"

Joe didn't say anything for a minute. Then he said, "Because I don't feel like going back."

"It doesn't make any difference what you feel like," I said. "We have to go back."

"You have to go back because he's your father," he said.

He was beginning to make me sore acting so great. "So?" I said. "He's your master, too."

He shook his head. "No, he isn't," he said. "Not any more. He didn't register me. I'm a free nigger now."

I didn't say anything for a minute. Then I said, "Joe, a little while ago I asked Father to set you free, but he wouldn't."

"That doesn't matter anymore, this is Pennsylvania now and I'm free."

"Joe, what good is it to be free? Where will you live? At least with us you've got a place to live."

He shook his head. "No, I don't," he said. "You don't even have the mill anymore. You'll have to go back to Connecticut."

"Maybe we won't go back. Maybe we'll build a new mill."

"No, you won't do that. Anyway you can have your damned mill. I just want to be free."

"Well, all right, you could come back to Connecticut with us."

"Back in Connecticut I'm not free anymore. I'm only free in Pennsylvania."

After that neither of us said anything. We just sat there in the high meadow listening to the roaring of the flood and watching the things bobbing on the water. Finally I said, "Come on back with me, Joe."

He didn't say anything.

"Please, Joe."

Suddenly he jumped up. "God damn it, Ben, you try being somebody's nigger for a while and see how you like it."

I jumped up, too. I knew he was right and I was wrong, and it was making me mad. "You don't have any right to be free, Joe."

"What do you mean, I don't—"

"My father paid for your food and your clothes and everything you have."

"What kind of a friend is that, Ben? What kind of a friend would want his friend to be a slave?"

"Well, what do you mean by running off?" I shouted. "What kind of a friend is that?"

"I don't want you for a friend anymore, Ben. I don't want anybody for a friend that won't let me be free. You say you would set me free when you grew up, but I bet you wouldn't."

"Yes, I would."

"Well, if you'll set me free then, why won't you let me be free now?"

"Because you aren't mine, you're Father's."

"The hell with him."

"All right," I shouted. "All right, if that's the way you want it."

"I don't want you for a friend anymore, Ben," he shouted. Then he swung around and hit me. In the dark he couldn't see very well, so his fist just bounced off my shoulder. I grabbed his arm and then we tumbled onto the cold wet ground and began to fight. We weren't fighting easy, either. We were sore and we kept twisting and turning, trying to get on top, and scratching ourselves all up on the cold grass. Suddenly we got loose from each other and stood facing, breathing in great gasps. And Joe Mountain, he was crying as hard as he could. "I don't want you for a friend anymore, Ben," he sobbed out. "I don't want you for a friend."

"All right," I shouted. I was crying too, and it was hard for me to talk. "All right."

We stood there, both of us trying to stop from crying and wishing we could be friends again. Finally I got my breath back a little. "Where are you going to go? What are you going to do?"

"I don't know," he said. "All I know is, I'm not going to be anybody's nigger anymore."

"You'll be sorry," I said.

"No, I won't," he said. "I'll never be sorry."

So I left. I turned and began to walk up the hill toward where we were camped. At the top of the high meadow I turned and looked back. I couldn't see much, but I could see the shape of Joe Mountain standing there in the dark. I couldn't tell which direction he was facing, whether he was looking at me or down at the flood. Then I turned around again and walked into the woods and out of sight of Joe Mountain. And all the way back to the camp I kept telling myself that Joe Mountain was wrong, that he shouldn't run off but should stay with us. But no matter what reasons I told myself in my head, someplace else inside me I knew that I was wrong, and that I'd wrecked it with my best friend.

8

In the morning the sun was shining bright, the air was warm and the birds were darting through the trees. We woke up when the sun was coming up, and Father and I walked down the hill, leaving Annie to guard our stuff. As we got into the high meadow we could see the Susquehanna. It was still flowing full, and over the banks in a lot of places, but mostly it was more or less back where it belonged. But it had left behind it pools and ponds and even lakes in the low places on the land that would take days to dry up.

The lower part of the meadow was covered with a

sheet of mud, with long, deep trenches cut into it where the water pouring out of the millpond had slashed at the earth. As we came up further we could see that the millrace was full of mud, and that a lot of the stones had been knocked out of its walls by the force of the water.

The mill was ruined. The waterwheel was gone completely. The stone walls of the cellar had held, although some of the top stones had been knocked off, but the rest of the mill was gone—just gone, as if it had never been there. The cellar was full of mud. We could see part of one millstone sticking up through the mud.

"Do you think the other one's down there, Father?"

"I hope so," he said. "A flood like that could carry a millstone off, but probably not as far as the river. I don't see it anywhere, so I guess it's down in the mud."

"I suppose the gears are all smashed up," I said.

He nodded. "Pretty sure to have got broken when the millstones dropped in there."

I sighed. "What are we going to do?"

He stared down into the mud filling the cellar. Then he looked at me. "Build it up again, of course."

"What?"

"What would you do, just give up?"

"Well." I thought about it. "I don't think Annie will want to stay here anymore."

He looked at me hard. "What do you think?"

"Father, Patterson's going to throw us out of the valley anyway. What's the sense of building him a mill? I think we should go back to Connecticut. Maybe it won't be as bad as we think back there. Maybe we could find another place that needed a mill. We could dig the millstones out, and the irons and take them with us. We've still got our tools, we've still got the oxen and the chickens."

He shook his head. "Patterson isn't going to be able to hang on here forever. He's got to feed those troops in the fort and where is he going to get food from now? He's going to have to buy it over at Sunbury, and I don't guess the Pennsylvania Assembly is going to sit still for that kind of expense too long."

"Father, you're just building up false hopes. What chance have we really got? Let's leave while we can still take the millstones and the irons. If we rebuild the mill Patterson will come and take the whole thing, and we won't have anything to take back except our clothes."

"No," he said. "No. We're not finished yet. As long as we've got a chance, we're staying here. Who knows, the Congress could give us back the land tomorrow. Zeb Butler has given up, but John Franklin has a plan for making this a separate state. And he's going to try to get us a hearing before Congress."

"Father, I have some say in this."

"I'm still boss here."

"I'm almost grown up. You can't run the mill without me, now that Joe's gone."

He didn't say anything, but looked down at the mud.

"Although maybe Joe will come back," I said. I knew I was just wishing.

"Be a damn fool if he did," Father said.

"I thought you said that niggers couldn't take care of themselves."

"Joe was different. He wasn't like most niggers. I should have known he'd run off sooner or later. He was too smart to be somebody's nigger all his life."

"Then why didn't you set him free?"

He spit down into the mud in the cellar. Then he looked up at the clear sky. "I began wondering that myself in the middle of the night when I came down here looking for him." He shook himself. "No use crying over spilt milk." He put his hand on my shoulder. "Ben, you're right, I need you. But I'm still boss. And we're staying."

I wasn't so sure that we were. I had a pretty good idea that Annie would want to run away, and if she did, I had a feeling I might go with her. Like she said, she needs a father for Little Isaac and a husband for herself, but there wasn't anything in the valley but old men, cripples, and widows.

But I didn't have a chance to think about it right then, because we had other things to do. We had a look at the house. Being farther away from the mill-pond it hadn't got the full force of the flood and it had held. But it was full of mud, and everything in-side—the beds, the chairs, everything—was soaking wet and muddy. The shed was all right, too. It had been pushed off its stone foundation, but we could fix that pretty easily, and anyway, nothing had to be done about it for the moment. So we spent the day carrying our things down from the woods, and clean-ing up the house, and by night time we'd got things organized enough so that we could cook a little johnnycake for supper, and sleep there.

A lot of other people hadn't been so lucky. It was pretty terrible. As close as anyone could figure a hundred and fifty farms up and down the valley had been washed away. Nobody knew how much live-stock had been drowned. Hundreds and thousands of cows and chickens and hogs and sheep were just gone, buried under mud or swept down the Sus-quehanna and out toward Chesapeake Bay. And, of course, the flood had ruined most of the crop of win-

ter rye, which would have been about ready to har-
vest. It had smashed up a lot of orchards, too, just
chewing the roots of the trees out of the ground and
then tipping them over, or washing them away completely. But the craziest thing was that the water had
actually taken away people's land—not just their
houses and livestock, but the dirt they grew things
in. You'd have places where all the beautiful topsoil
was washed right out of the cornfield, leaving
nothing but a great space of sand. Then the topsoil
would be dumped down on somebody else's place as
a huge heap of mud, so that the farmer would have to
spend days getting his land leveled so that he could
plant on it. In other places the creeks and streams cut
new beds, changing their courses completely, so that
part of your land might suddenly be on the other
side of a creek, and then the question was—
whose land was it? Even crazier were the great big
chunks of ice that had been frozen in the rivers. A lot
of them ended up on land, some of them enormous,
as big as wagons, as big as sheds. Some people's fields
were entirely covered with ice, just blocks and blocks
of it everywhere, and it's hard to believe, but some
were so big that they lasted all summer: even in Sep-
tember there were still small pieces of them left lying
in the fields.

But the worst damage was done right along the

banks of the Susquehanna where the trees had been cut off. Just the way Father had said, there was nothing there to hold the banks and they just washed away. Fifteen, twenty yards back from the river it was all rocks and gravel, with great gulleys in it running down to the river. Acres and acres of land had been lost—it was gone down the river and out to sea. In fact, some islands that had been in the middle of the Susquehanna had disappeared, too. Oh, it's just amazing how powerful a thing like a flood can be. I know of houses that were swept away and traveled on the flood for six or seven miles. Even a stone house, forty feet long, got moved along a little ways by the flood. It's hard to believe such a thing could happen, but it did.

Rebuilding houses, though, wasn't so much of a problem. There was plenty of wood around to work with and with warm weather coming, you could camp outside for a while anyway. The main problem was food. There just wasn't much left. Some people, whose farms were back farther up in the hills were all right, but most people had built in the bottom land along the river where the soil was so good, and they'd lost their grain, their livestock, and everything else. There wouldn't be any new corn until the first crop came in around July. The only place where there was any food to amount to anything was in the fort.

In the fort they had grain; and the question was, would they give us any or let us starve? We were lucky about one thing: we'd saved Father's Brown Bess and powder and shot, so at least we'd be able to hunt. There was enough game in the woods to keep us going, if we could find it, and as soon as the river got back to normal there'd be fish in it again.

So even though it seemed like we could get back on our feet again if we worked night and day for the rest of the summer, just as I figured, Annie didn't want any part of it. She waited until dinner that first night to bring it up. We were pretty tired, just sitting there eating our johnnycake, and she brought it up. "All right, Father," she said. "Now we're going back."

Father didn't look up from his food. I guess he knew it was coming. "We'll talk about it tomorrow, Annie. We're all too tired to discuss it tonight."

"There's nothing to discuss," she said. "We're going, that's all. We'll stay just long enough to get the millstones up out of the mud and loaded onto the wagons, and then we're going."

"Since when are you giving the orders around here?"

"I'm not giving orders, Father, I'm stating a fact. We're going back to Connecticut. It won't take you and Ben more than three or four days to get the millstones up, and everything packed. Then we're leaving."

"Father," I said, "I think Annie's right. It isn't worth it anymore. Patterson's just going to take the place anyway."

"Ben," Annie said, "don't even argue with him. We're going."

"We'll talk about it in the morning," Father said.

"There's nothing to talk about."

"Annie, I'm not taking orders from you yet."

She jumped up from the table and her chair tipped over behind her. "What's the matter with you, Father? Can't you see that we're finished here? Don't you know that Patterson's going to drive us out? What are you waiting for, until we all get shot or drowned or starved to death?" She was so angry she was crying and the words were choking in her mouth. "What kind of man are you to risk your family just to save your precious mill?"

"I am running this family, and you will do as I say."

She began to cry harder, so angry that she was shaking. "I'm not going to let Little Isaac get killed like his father was." She went outside into the dark.

The next morning Father took the Brown Bess out into the forest to see if he could get a deer. Annie began spreading things out in the sun to dry, and I took a shovel down into the mill, and began cleaning the mud out of it. I had been down there for about an hour when Annie came along. She stood at the top looking down at me. "You look like the tar baby."

"I guess I might just as well dive in the river with my clothes on to get clean," I said.

She watched for a minute. Then she said, "Ben, I'm going back to Connecticut. I'm taking Little Isaac and I'm going back."

"Did you tell Father?"

"No. I'm not going to tell him. He'd try to stop me. I'm just going to go."

"Where will you go to?"

She shrugged. "Uncle John's, I guess."

"And work for him?"

"It's better than being murdered and flooded out and starved. Besides, back there I might get married again."

"You'd have a better chance, I reckon. Lot more widows out here than spare men."

"Anyway, it doesn't matter about getting married. I just want to live someplace where I don't have to worry all the time. How can I raise Little Isaac right out here?"

"I don't think it's hurting him any," I said.

"I'd like him to get some schooling," she said.

"Look at you, you've only had enough schooling so's you can read and write and cipher a little."

"Well, I know," I said, "I'd like to get more schooling. Father said that someday, if we get a little bit ahead, he'd send me over to the academy in Windham."

"That's one of Father's big ifs," she said. "We're not getting ahead; we're getting behind."

I didn't say anything.

"Ben, I think you ought to come with me."

"Father wants me to stay."

"He can't make you stay—you're near a grown-up now."

"I'm fifteen."

"That's grown-up enough," she said.

"I don't know," I said. "Maybe."

"I think you ought to."

"When are you going?"

"Soon," she said. "I'm going to ask around and see if anybody's going back that's got room in a wagon. I've got to collect up some food, too—just enough for us to eat on the way. Some flour and dried meat and such."

"I don't know," I said. "Maybe."

I thought about it while I dug the mud out of the cellar over the next few days. I couldn't make up my mind. On one side of it, it seemed to me pretty clear that Patterson was going to take over the whole place pretty soon. It didn't seem worthwhile rebuilding the mill just so he could take it over. Since the flood he'd been pretty busy going around and finding out which people were giving up and going back, so he could take over their farms when they left. Sooner or later he'd get to us, I figured.

But on the other side of it, I was sort of scared of going against Father. I don't know why that should be so, but it was. I mean if I left, there wouldn't be anything he could do about it. Back in Connecticut if a son went off without permission you might be able to get a Justice of the Peace to arrest him and bring him back to his father until he was twenty-one; but out here the only Justice of the Peace was Patterson, and he wasn't likely to keep any Connecticut people from leaving. So there wasn't much Father could do about it if I decided to leave. But still, he'd been my boss all my life; it was hard going against him.

Anyway, I didn't have to decide until Annie was ready to go. In the meanwhile, I figured I'd try to put aside a little food for myself, just in case. I was doing some fishing every day. Patterson had made it illegal to fish, but we did it anyway. We had to. We ate some of the fish; but if there was extra I'd dry it in the sun and salt it down in a barrel. You could live a long time on salt fish if you had to.

I went on cleaning up the mill. I got enough mud dug out so that we could get to the stones, and then we got a couple of people to come and help us get them out. We set up a plank ramp leading down into the cellar, hitched the oxen to the stone, and then while Father drove the oxen, the rest of us got down in the cellar and prised it up, so as to help the oxen with the weight and keep it on the ramp. It didn't take us too long to get them out. They were in pretty good shape. The upper stone had a big chunk broke out of its edge where it had smashed down on the nether stone, but it would work well enough.

The shafts and gears, though, were pretty much of a mess. I got the pieces up, washed them out in the millstream, and salvaged what I could. There'd be a lot of work to do on them. The biggest problem, though, was building the mill itself.

Father and I talked about it. "I'm going to have to leave a lot of it to you," he said. "I'll be spending a good deal of time hunting for the moment."

It kind of pleased me to have charge of rebuilding the mill. It was more interesting than most other kinds of work, and I liked it. Besides, it made me feel good at the end of the day when I could look around at the timbers I'd hewed or the planks I'd sawed, and see what I'd accomplished. So for the first week or so that's what I did. I got timbers adzed square for sills around the tops of the cellar walls, and then I began laying down a puncheon floor—just logs split in half, laid down with their split sides up, and pegged at the ends into the sills. For that time we lived on what Father could shoot. But we needed grain, too, and so after a week or so he said to me, "They've got grain up at the fort, I'm going to see if they can spare us some."

"They won't do that," I said. "They'd just as soon drive us out."

"Patterson would, he'd stop at nothing to drive us out. But there's some up there who don't like to see people starve. A couple of men have been up there and got grain. They weren't supposed to get any—they've been stopping people from getting into the commissary with bayonets. But Peter Obersheimer, the man in charge, doesn't want to see people starve and he'll slip you a little grain if he can. If they want us to rebuild the mill they've got to feed us."

It seemed reasonable when he put it that way, but I didn't trust it. Patterson wasn't the helpful kind. But Father figured it was worth a chance. "The worst they can do is say no," he said. So he hitched up the wagon and rode out, leaving me to work on the mill.

I'd got the floor laid; and the next job was to make a waterwheel. Once we had the wheel made we could repair the machinery, then put the stones back in place, and we could operate the mill. Of course there'd be no walls or roof and we'd only be able to run the mill in dry weather—you couldn't take a chance on getting the flour wet—but it would be a start. We could build the millhouse itself later.

Making a waterwheel isn't easy. It had to be twelve feet high, like the old one, and it had to fit in exactly the same space. My first job was to make two twelve-foot wheels, more or less like regular wagon wheels, only a lot bigger. To make a wheel you start by making a hub out of a round block maybe four inches in diameter and six inches long. You drill holes in this and fit spokes into the holes. My spokes would have to be pretty near six feet long. Then you make the wheel itself in sections, maybe two feet long, each with just the right curve in it. You drill a hole in the inside part of the curve of each section, fit the sections onto the spokes, and then peg the sections together with little pegs. When you're remaking a wagon wheel you finish it off with a band of thin iron, bending it into a circle, and riveting the ends together, so you have an iron tire just big enough to fit around the wheel. You heat the tire so it expands, then slip it over the wooden wheel. When the tire cools, it shrinks and pulls everything tightly together. But for the mill wheel we wouldn't use an iron tire. The paddles that ran between the two big wheels would hold everything together pretty well.

I spent the morning shaping my hub and drilling the spoke holes in it. It was pretty interesting work, and I didn't notice how the time was going until Annie came out to get me for my noon meal, which was rabbit stew. "I wish we had some bread to go with it," she said.

"I don't guess very many people are eating bread with their stew these days."

"Probably not. Where's Father?"

"He went up to the fort to see if they'd give us some grain. What time is it?"

"About noon."

"He should have been back a long while ago," I said.

She shrugged. "It's a crazy idea, anyway. Patterson isn't going to give us any grain."

"I don't guess so," I said.

I ate my dinner and drank some cider. It was about all we had to drink. The flood had ruined most of the wells close to the river and anybody who had beer was lucky. We usually had a few barrels of cider around, and maybe some rum or whiskey too, because sometimes people would pay us in things like that for milling their grain.

I finished my meal and went back to work shaping my spokes. I got occupied with the work and suddenly I realized that two or three more hours had gone by and Father still hadn't come back. It worried me: there wasn't any reason for him to stay up at the fort so long. I tried to think whether I ought to go down there and see what the matter was; but then I realized that if he'd gotten into some kind of trouble up there, the best thing for me to do was to stay away. If I got into trouble myself, there'd be nobody left at the mill to look after Annie and Little Isaac.

Father came back just at dusk. I didn't have to get but one look at him sitting on the wagon to realize that something was wrong. He wasn't sitting up straight the way he usually did, but was slumped over the seat as if he could hardly keep awake. I dropped the spoke shave and ran across the mill yard to help him. He was really a mess. His face was smeared with mud, there was a big cut across his forehead and a trickle of dried blood coming out of his nose.

"What happened?"

"Get me a glass of rum, Ben."

I looked into the wagon. It was empty. I helped him down from the seat and then I ran into the house and shouted, "Little Isaac, bring Father some rum." Then I went back to the wagon. Father was sitting on the mill floor. "What happened?"

"They beat hell out of me. Unhitch the oxen and take them up into the meadow." I got the oxen loose and drove them up into the high meadow. They were glad to get up there and graze. Then I came back down into the mill yard. When I got there Father was still sitting on the puncheon floor, drinking a cup of rum and talking to Annie and Little Isaac.

"They've got maybe twenty Connecticut men locked up in there now. They picked them up on all sorts of excuses—any reason they could think of. Once they get the men off the farms, they run the women and children out and take over." He looked around and spat. "Looks like a pretty good job on those spokes, Ben."

"Did they beat you, Father?"

"They sure as hell did," he said. "I didn't get these cuts falling down."

"How did it happen?"

"Well, I went into the fort and up to the head-quarters and asked for Commissioner Montgomery. There were a bunch of these Rangers hanging around. They sure are poor examples of soldiers, but I guess that's the best they can get to come out here. They don't shave, none of them, and some of them were pretty drunk. They asked me what I wanted to see Montgomery for, and I said I was trying to get grain for my family, and they just began to push me around. Well, I lost my temper, which I shouldn't have done, and a couple of them grabbed me and held me while another one punched me in the face.

Then when they'd had enough fun out of that and were getting bored, they threw me into the blockhouse. That was all there was to it."

"What's it like in the blockhouse, Grandpa?" Little Isaac asked.

"It's not so nice, Isaac. Just a muddy floor and about twenty men standing around, some of them sick and all of them hungry."

Annie looked at him. "And now will you go back, Father?"

He rubbed his hand across his face and sighed. "Don't start that please, Annie," he said. "I've had enough for one day."

"Father, I just can't understand it. I just can't understand why people would do something like that just for no reason."

He sighed. "They're trying to drive us out, Ben. They want to make it so hard for us that we'll just get out on our own."

Father went to bed early that night, and Annie and I walked out to the mill and sat on the puncheon floor, talking. "Made up your mind yet?" she said.

"I don't guess things are going to get any better," I said. "I hate to leave the mill though, just when we're getting it back in order."

"What difference does that make?" she said. "Patterson's going to take it anyway."

"Maybe he won't," I said.

"He will."

"When are you planning to go?"

"After warm weather. When the rivers are a little lower. Maybe in May."

"What about food?"

"I've been drying some venison."

"What?" I said. "You've been holding back on the meat?"

She got red. "I'm entitled to it."

"Father would be furious if he knew."

"I don't care," she said. "I don't care about Father. Little Isaac comes first."

I didn't say anything. I knew how she felt. "Well, I don't know," I said. "I guess probably I'll go. It's the only sensible thing." I ran my hand through my hair. "I sure hate to leave the mill, though, just when it's going right."

We went on working on the mill. There'd be grain coming in soon from the farmers who had winter rye growing on high land. We finished the waterwheel, and then we started repairing the shafts and gears. Father worked with me sometimes, but I worked on the mill a lot by myself. The truth was, it was more my mill than it was his. A lot of times there'd be some decision to make, about where to fit the gears or how the shaft should run, and I'd make the decision myself, instead of waiting until I could talk to Father. I was proud of that.

Finally the waterwheel was done and some men came and helped us put it in place. We blocked it up on logs so it was just where we wanted it, and began hitching it to the machinery. Once that was done we could set the stones in place, and we'd be ready to operate. There was still the main building itself to be put up and all the machinery for feeding grain in, which would take the rest of the summer. But in the meantime we could at least grind.

So April went along. Things weren't getting any better. Every few days we'd hear about some new farmer that Patterson had arrested. It was terrible. A lot of the men saw clearly enough that they were going to be arrested eventually, too, and some of them had even left their farms and were living in caves and camps out in the forest. The idea was that Patterson wouldn't arrest women and children. They could keep the farms going, and the men would hide out in the forest, hoping that sooner or later Congress would get into it, or the Pennsylvania government would get tired of supporting the Rangers and order Patterson to disband them.

Then one morning late in the month, as I was adzing some timbers, I heard the sound of horses. It was a beautiful sunny day, and I felt pretty good. The horses were coming up the road from Wilkes-Barre toward the mill. I stopped adzing and stood there in the mill yard watching them come up.

Three of them were Rangers carrying clubs, and one was Alexander Patterson. My heart began to race.

"You Buck?" Patterson asked.

"Yes, sir," I said.

"You're holding a nigger up here illegally," he said. He took a piece of paper out of his saddle bag and looked at it. "A nigger named Joe Mountain."

"He isn't here anymore," I said. "He ran off."

"He ran off?"

"Yes, sir," I said. "During the flood. We haven't seen him since."

"That the truth?" Patterson said.

"Yes, sir."

"I don't believe it. Where's your father?"

I knew where he was; he'd taken the wagon out to a farmer toward Capouse, to bring in some grain for milling. "He went hunting," I said.

"Where?"

"I don't know," I said. "Usually he hunts upback," I said pointing in the opposite direction from where Father was.

Then I heard the rumbling of wagon wheels and squeaking of an axle. I looked down the road. Father was coming up the hill with the wagon. I dropped my adze. Patterson and the Rangers were between me and the road. I took a breath and then dashed forward, hoping to slip by the horses. "Stand still, boy," Patterson shouted. I darted between two horses. "Father," I shouted. Then something hit me from behind and I fell down into the dirt. There were sounds of horses wheeling, and then the wagon sounds stopped, and I sat up, feeling the back of my head. My hand came away wet. There was blood on it. One of the Rangers had hit me with his club, I figured. I felt dizzy, and I just went on sitting there in the dirt.

Father had come up on the wagon and had stopped in the road before the mill yard. Patterson had drawn up to him on his horse. They sat facing each other. "Where's that nigger you had here, Buck?"

Father shrugged. "I don't know. He's gone."

Patterson jerked his head toward the house. "Have a look inside." One of the Rangers climbed down from his horse and went into the house. "You say he's gone, Buck, we'll find out."

In a couple of minutes the Ranger came back. "There's no nigger in there," he said. "Just a woman and a kid."

"All right, Buck," Patterson said. "Where is he?"

"I told you I don't know. He ran away."

"When did he go off?"

"The night of the flood. He saw his chance and he left. We haven't seen him since."

"I don't believe you," Patterson said. "I believe you sold him. That's illegal under Pennsylvania law."

"Now, Mr. Patterson," my father said, "who would I sell a nigger to around here? There isn't enough cash between here and Easton to buy a couple of hens, much less a nigger. That's just foolish."

"We'll see how foolish it is. I'm placing you under arrest."

Father stared at him for a minute and I knew he was trying to figure what chance he would have if he jumped off the wagon and ran for it. They'd have a hard time following him in the forest if he could make it that far; but first he'd have to get through the high meadow. "Well," he said finally, "I don't see how you can arrest me unless you've got some evidence. And I don't see that you've got any."

"You were holding an unregistered nigger slave up here, and that's illegal. That's evidence enough for me."

My father leaned over and spit into the dirt. "It doesn't much seem like I was holding him, does it now."

"Arrest him, constable."

My father held up his hand. "Hold it a minute," he said. "Just suppose you throw me into the fort.

Who's going to do your milling for you?"

"You're not the only miller in the world."

"I'm the only one around here."

"Not any more, you're not," Patterson said. "There's a miller coming in from Philadelphia next week. I think he'll do just fine."

"You bastard," my father said. "You waited until we had the mill working, before you took it over, didn't you? That's my mill, Patterson. I dragged those stones two hundred miles from Connecticut, I scraped my hands bloody on those rocks building that dam, I built that mill up from the ground once and now my boy's doing it a second time. What right have you got to take it away from me?"

"Nobody calls me a bastard and gets away with it, Buck."

"You're a bastard, Patterson."

"That's resisting arrest. Take him, constable."

Father leaped from the wagon, sprang over the fence into the high meadow, and began zig-zagging up through the field toward the forest at the top. Patterson jerked a pistol from his belt, leveled it across his arm, and fired. At the same time, the Rangers wheeled their horses around, backed off from the fence thirty feet, and then charged for it. But the horses wouldn't jump.

"Open that gate, boy," Patterson shouted, turning

the pistol toward me. I jumped to my feet, and ran to the gate. It was fastened by a wooden pin which ran through two iron loops. I jerked at the pin, pretending it was stuck. Patterson jumped from the horse, knocked me away from the gate, jerked the pin out, and swung the gate open. The two Rangers charged through it and up the meadow, waving their clubs. Patterson swung around, rested his pistol barrel on the top rail of the fence, sighted and fired. Then he reloaded swearing. Father was still running, maybe fifty yards from the woods. Once more Patterson fired. Father kept on running. The horsemen were closing in on him fast. Patterson reloaded again. Father was only ten yards from the woods. Patterson fired again. Father disappeared into the forest, and the horsemen reined up.

9

Now I knew it was time to leave the valley and suddenly I didn't want to go. It surprised me to feel that way. I guess a lot of it had to do with the new mill. I'd built it myself—or at least most of it. Of course, Father had done a lot of the work, and we'd had help from the neighbors to get the waterwheel up and the stones in place. But I'd done most of it—built the wheel and repaired the machinery and laid the floor—and when I got done with it, the mill worked. The waterwheel turned, the gears meshed, the stones went around. I wasn't just somebody's son, I was a real miller. I could do something most people couldn't do. And I didn't want to give it all up to go back to Connecticut and work on Uncle John's farm for the rest of my life.

But now Father was gone, and who knew what had happened to him. After Patterson and his people had left I had gone up into the high meadow to see if I could find traces of blood. I didn't see anything, but that didn't mean too much: I could have been looking in the wrong place. So I had walked a good way into the forest, but still there were no signs of blood, or of Father either. Who knew where he was?

There was one thing for sure: Annie was going to leave. And I knew I'd have to go with her. How could I let her trek all the way back to Connecticut by herself, with Little Isaac to take care of?

We talked about it that first night after Patterson ran Father off. We were sitting around the table. "We better not waste any time," Annie said. "We'd better go as soon as we can."

I didn't say anything.

"You don't think you can stay, do you?"

"I don't know," I said. "I hate to leave now, after I did all that work on the mill."

"I told you and Father not to build it up again," she said. "I told you Patterson would get it anyway. We should have gone back weeks ago. Then maybe we'd still have Father."

"I don't think he's dead," I said. "There are a lot of men back up in the woods waiting to see if the troops leave. Father's probably up there with them."

"That's fine," she said. "That's just fine. And so there'll be another battle and people getting killed, and maybe Father, too. If he isn't dead already."

"I don't think he's dead. He didn't stumble or fall or anything if any ball hit him. I don't think he got a bad wound."

"But we don't know."

I didn't say anything for a minute. I knew she was right, but I didn't want to go. "I wish we could talk to Father before we decided."

"I've already decided, Ben. Little Isaac and I are going, and if you won't go with us, we'll go alone."

"You'd walk all the way back to Connecticut by yourself?"

"I've been talking with some other women. There's three or four will go."

"And what about food?" I said.

"I've got enough dried meat to last until we get to Shohola. People will help us there. We'll beg if we have to."

"When are you thinking about going?"

"I don't know," she said. "In a couple of days, probably."

"And what about your clothes and the dishes and the pots and pans?"

"We'll take what we can," she said. "We'll leave the rest."

"The tools? The millstones?"

"You should have thought of that sooner. If we'd have gone right after the flood we could have taken it all in the wagons. Since you've got the mill rebuilt you just know that Patterson isn't going to let you take anything."

I knew that she was right. We'd have to go. "I still wish we could talk to Father," I said. "He might have some ideas."

"There isn't any way, Ben. Don't feel bad. You tried, you did your best, but you can't fight an army. They've won."

Oh, I felt bad. I felt cheated; what right had Patterson and his men to drive us out of there, after we'd worked so hard to build something? That was *my* mill, it wasn't their mill. Oh, I was angry. I'd have been glad to shoot Patterson if I thought I could get away with it.

But there wasn't any hope of that, and anyway, it wouldn't do any good. The only thing to do was swallow it, pack up our stuff, and go. So the next day I began trying to figure out what to take. What I really wanted to do was take the oxen and a wagon. We'd have room enough in the wagon to take all of our clothes and the things from the house, as well as a lot of the tools. But that seemed pretty risky. The oxen traveled pretty slow, a lot slower than we could move on foot. Patterson wouldn't have any trouble catching up to us, even after we'd been traveling for two or three days. On foot we could always duck off into the woods if we heard horses. I didn't think Patterson would stop us if we went on foot. He wanted us to leave, so long as we didn't take anything too valuable from the mill.

So we began getting ready. Annie gathered together as much flour as she could find and baked it into loaves of bread. We wrapped the bread, the dried meat Annie had been saving and the salted fish I'd saved up, in a cloth. "It doesn't seem like much," Annie said.

"We may be able to shoot some game along the way," I said. "It's going to take us about seven days to get out of the valley and over to Shohola. Once we get there we'll find food."

It didn't take long to get ready. There wasn't that much to pack. A day later we were set, but still I didn't want to leave. We ate a little dinner at noon, and then I went out to the mill and stood there on the puncheon floor I'd spent so much time laying. The sun was shining, Mill Creek was sort of drifting along in a quiet and peaceful way. There were fish flashing around in it. It was hard to say good-bye. I'd spent eight years in the valley. A lot had happened; it was my life.

I went back into the house. "I think we ought to wait until morning," I said. "I think we ought to leave a couple of hours before sunup. That way we can get well up the valley before light." It was a good excuse, but it wasn't the truth: I just wanted to stay a little longer.

We went to bed early that night, Annie up in the loft and me in the shed as usual. It was still dark when I woke up. I could hear somebody moving around. I got out of bed and went from the shed into the main room. "Annie?"

"It's me."

"Father?" He'd kicked the fire up a little bit and he was sitting in front of it. In the red glow his face was tired, and he hadn't shaved for a while. His clothes were dirty, too. "Are you all right?"

"I'm all right," he said. "Just hungry."

Annie was coming down the ladder. "Father, are you all right?" she said.

"I'm all right."

"Where have you been?" Annie said.

"A bunch of us are living up in the hills. There's some caves up there."

"What are you doing for food?"

"There's game. We get by."

Nobody said anything for a minute. Annie and I stood in front of the fire, looking at Father. Finally Annie said, "We're going back, Father."

He nodded. "I heard. That's why I came down."

"We're going pretty soon," Annie said. "As soon as it starts to get light. We're all packed."

He sat there for a minute. Then he said, "I don't want you to go. I want you to stay."

Annie didn't say anything. "Father," I said, "I want to stay, but there's no use."

"Patterson's about finished. The Pennsylvania Assembly has finally realized that he's been breaking the law out here. He's not supposed to be putting people out on his own say-so. We've got word from a fellow who was at the fort that the Assembly is pretty well fed up with the whole thing. They're tired of paying for the Rangers, for one thing, and they've ordered Patterson to disband at the end of the month. He hasn't got much time left. All we have to do is wait it out."

"No," Annie said. "No. There's going to be another war, I know it."

"There won't be a war if the Rangers go," Father said. "How can they fight without troops? I want you both to stay here."

"Annie," I said.

"No," she said. "No, no, no."

"Father, if Annie goes I have to go with her. I can't let her and Little Isaac walk all that way by themselves."

"Annie's not going," he said. "You're both staying."

"You can't keep me here, Father."

"Father," I said, "if Annie decides to go, she'll go."

He sat still and said nothing. Then he said, "No, I guess she will."

We were silent. Then he said, "All right, I can't order you to stay. I'm asking you to stay. Just till the end of the month. If Patterson doesn't go by then, I won't keep you here any longer. I won't ask you to stay. But we think he's going, and we think after that the valley will be ours. So I'm asking you to stay."

I waited. Annie said nothing. "It's up to Annie," I said. "I'll stay, but it's up to her."

"All right," she said. She looked like she was going to cry. "Till the end of the month. That's all."

"Thank you, Annie," Father said. He stood up. "I have to leave before daylight."

Annie crossed the room to where our packages of food were sitting by the door. "You may as well eat something before you go," she said.

He ate some dried beef and some bread, and then he left, and we went back to bed. I was feeling better. I didn't really believe that Patterson would leave; but there was a chance. In the morning I'd start on the mill again. It was probably a waste of time, but at least it was a hopeful thing to do.

And I was out in the mill, working on a timber for

the walls, when I heard horses' hooves. I looked up. It was Patterson and a couple of the Rangers coming up the road. My first idea was to run for it. But I didn't: I stood there waiting. The three men rode into the mill yard. Annie heard the sound and came out of the house, with Little Isaac just behind her. She stood in the doorway watching. The horsemen reined up. Patterson reached into his saddlebag, and drew out some papers. "Buck, I have a court order here demanding that you vacate these premises forthwith."

I stared at him. "This is my mill," I said.

"Not anymore it isn't. I'm taking it over. We're clearing the valley of Yankees today. All of you, every last one."

And that was the way it was. Patterson was desperate. In two weeks the troops would be withdrawn. He had tried to starve us out, he tried jailing the men, and we had stuck. And now he was going to run us out with guns. I sat in the house with Annie, my head down on the table. I wanted to cry, but I couldn't—I felt too bitter.

"Ben," Annie said softly, "we couldn't have lasted. There's nobody left in the valley but women and children anyway. How could we have survived? The men are in jail or out in the woods hiding in caves like Father."

"We could have tried," I said.

"It wouldn't have worked."

We started out the next morning, carrying what we could on our backs. Patterson had demanded that we take the upper road, which went up through the hills, instead of the lower road along the river. The upper road was overgrown in places and there were no bridges across the streams. We'd have to ford each one.

"He's hoping to kill us all on the trip," I said.

"I know," Annie said. "Some will die, that's sure. Some of the women are pregnant. There's small children, there's old men, and cripples."

We walked into Wilkes-Barre and there we found the women and children gathered in small groups. We had no leaders, no organization. We just began to move slowly toward the upper road, heading north toward Capouse Meadows. There were five hundred of us all told, being driven out of the valley that had been our home like dried leaves before a cold November wind. We were all on foot. A lot of the people still had carts and wagons, but they'd eaten the oxen. Even if we'd been able to take out carts and wagons, it wouldn't have mattered, because with the upper road overgrown and so many creeks to ford, it wasn't worth the trouble to try to push a cart through. And coming along behind us, just to keep us moving, were some Rangers on horseback.

There was sixty-five miles to go and by myself I'd have been able to do it in three days, easy. But a pregnant woman couldn't go that fast, or a crippled man, or a little child. I doubted if we could do better than ten miles a day; that meant a week on the road, and what were we going to eat?

All day we struggled along over the rough road. Once it had been a good cart path, but now it was full of saplings and brush. Some of us who were stronger went up to the front and tried to trample down a path in the brush for the weaker ones coming along behind. That helped some; but still, it wasn't easy for a crippled man to get through. The worst thing, though, was watching some mother with one little baby in her arms and a couple of more small ones sort of hanging onto her skirts as they went along. Of course they were hungry—we all were. The kids would whimper and about every little while say something about food. But you couldn't explain to the kids that they'd have to be hungry for a while. You couldn't explain that to a baby, and so the baby would be crying and you'd see the mother trying to calm the baby down as she walked along, and then maybe losing her temper because there wasn't anything she could do about it.

We spent the night at a place called Capouse

Meadows, where there was a cleared space to camp in. There wasn't any problem about wood for fires— there was plenty around—but there wasn't much to cook over them. A few people had small bags of flour they'd managed to save, or maybe dried apples or pears left over from winter. One woman had a goat she was leading along on a string, and one of the crippled men had two chickens. He'd wrapped cloths around their heads to keep them quiet, tied their feet together and was carrying them along slung over his shoulders. But the chickens and the goat wouldn't go very far among us—for of course they'd share. We didn't have much more than the rest of them, either, just the dried meat, the salted fish and a few small loaves of bread. We made a fire, and ate some of the meat and bread. It wasn't much, but it would give us strength to keep going the next day.

Of course there was another problem: we didn't know where we were going to. There weren't many towns along the Delaware big enough to take on five hundred extra mouths, and besides, none of us had any money, or very little, anyway. We'd just have to throw ourselves on the mercy of people and hope that they'd be able to spare some food for us.

The next morning we hit the first of the creeks we had to ford. We came over the brow of a hill and there it was down at the bottom, about fifty feet wide, and rushing from the spring rains. As soon as we saw it we stopped and looked down at it. It looked pretty deep. I wished Father were there. We needed some leader to tell us what to do. But I'd been swimming in Mill Creek for years, and I figured it wouldn't be any problem for me to try it first. So I said, just sort of to everybody, "I'll go down and see how deep it is. Come on, Little Isaac."

We walked down the brushy, sloping road to the bottom. The creek was high, running only a few inches below its bank. I took off my clothes and laid them down on the ground, and then I stepped out into the water. It was swift and oh my, it was cold. A couple of feet in the bank sloped down sharply, and all of a sudden I was up to my waist. I stopped and cautiously eased my foot forward on the stony creek bottom. Still it went down, and so that in a few more steps the freezing water was up to my shoulders. I kept going cautiously out. The water was moving fast and I had trouble keeping my balance. It was going to be tough for a lot of the older people to make it across. A lot of them didn't know how to swim. I went on plowing through and suddenly the creek bed began to rise and in a minute I was on the other side, catching my breath and shivering in the sunlight. The sun began to dry me. I didn't want to have to get myself wet all over again, but I dove into the creek and swam back over, going as fast as I could. Then I dried with a handful of grass.

"Is it cold?" Little Isaac said.

"Damn right it is," I said.

"I don't like cold water," he said.

I got dressed and went back up the slope to where the rest were waiting. They were talking among themselves, and they were worried. "We're going to make a chain," Annie told me. "The big ones will have to carry the children across."

So the whole bunch moved down to the water. Nobody undressed. The women were too modest for that. They formed a chain, a couple of the biggest women going first, and started to string out across the creek. I put Little Isaac on my shoulders. I grabbed the hand of the person ahead of me, holding Little Isaac with the other hand. Annie grabbed onto my belt from behind, and gave her free hand to the person in back of her. We moved slowly across the water. So long as everybody held tight nobody could be swept away in the current. A couple of times I twisted around to see how things were going behind us, but with Little Isaac on my back it was hard to see much, so I kept plowing on ahead, carefully feeling with my feet for holes and stones so I wouldn't stumble and drop Little Isaac into the water. About five minutes later we were on the other side.

I put Little Isaac down and looked around. There were about fifteen people strung out across the creek with their arms spread, like a row of wooden puppets. Behind them the others waited their turn. For some it wasn't much of a problem to get across; but for crippled men and pregnant women and the women with little children, it was a bad business. A healthy woman could carry a child across all right; but they weren't all healthy and most of them were hungry or even downright starving.

I stood on the bank, watching. A lot of the babies were crying—they didn't like it when the cold water splashed up on them. I kept looking around, trying to keep an eye on the ones I thought were going to have trouble making it across. I was worried about one woman who had two small children and was pregnant with a third. She was standing by the bank, sort of waiting her turn, and I could tell she wasn't in any hurry to get started. A couple of other women were talking to her. She was sort of shaking, as if she already felt the cold of the water, and suddenly I realized that she was scared and crying. The other two women went on talking to her for a minute. Then one of them picked up the littlest of the children, a boy I judged to be about three, and put him on his mother's shoulders. Another woman picked up the other child, a girl of six. Then the third woman picked up her own child, and the three of them linked themselves to the human chain and stepped out into the water—three women with children on their backs.

They came across slowly. I could see by the way they were moving that they were feeling along the bottom of the creek with their feet for stones and holes. The kids were scared and hanging on tightly. The two older children had their arms around the women's shoulders, but the little three-year-old boy being carried by his pregnant mother kept putting his arms over her face to get a grip, and she kept having to let go of the woman in front of her to snatch his hand off her eyes.

And then all of a sudden they disappeared. I don't know what happened, but one minute the three women were coming across the creek with the children on their shoulders and the next minute they were gone, sunk down beneath the water. One of them had tripped, probably; but there was no way to tell. I started running toward the creek bank. One of the women appeared above the water, struggling to stand up. In a couple of seconds the other two women appeared, and with them the two older children. But the little boy was not in sight, and his mother was shrieking. I hit the river bank, dove straight in, and began swimming with my head up out of the water so I could look around. There was no little head bobbing in the current. I stopped swimming and stood, staring downstream. I saw nothing but the swift water; and then I saw a flash of something, a bit of white, a curl of foam, I didn't know what. I plunged back into the freezing water and began to swim as hard as I could, still keeping my head up so I could see. Every moment or two I would see the flash and then it would disappear again. I plunged on. Some of the women were running along the bank shouting and pointing. The flash came and went. I closed in on it but I was fifty yards downstream before I caught up to it.

The boy was floating face down. I grabbed him by the shirt and jerked him out of the stream. His eyes were opened and staring and his blonde hair was dripping water. I threw him over my shoulder. The water poured out of his mouth in a stream—maybe a quart of it. Then I carried him to shore. The mother went kind of crazy. She hugged him and hugged him and kept calling his name—"Johnny, Johnny, Johnny," and for a long time she wouldn't let go of him. But finally the other women got him away from her. We buried him in a shallow hole—we didn't have anything much to dig with—and put a log over the grave. Then we walked on.

10

That night the wolves came. We were camped in a meadow in a place called Cobbs. Annie and Little Isaac and I had eaten some bread and dried meat, and then we'd laid down to sleep by the side of the fire. We had no blankets and even though the days were nice and warm, the nights were cold. We were pretty tired. We weren't getting enough to eat; and I knew that in a few days we'd begin to get low on food. I'd have to figure something out—do some fishing, or set some rabbit snares if I could find a trail. I was lying there thinking about that and staring at the stars when the wolves began to howl.

Oh, it was an awful noise, a kind of deep bark and then long, long cries. Another one answered, and then another. We all sat up.

"What's that?" Little Isaac asked.

"Wolves," I said.

"Will they come after us?"

"No, they won't attack a group of people. They'll stay away."

"Then what are they howling about? Why don't they go away?"

I didn't say anything. I knew that they were after sick stragglers, and I was afraid to think of what they'd already got. I wished we'd buried him deeper, but it was too late to wish that now. "They're just howling, Little Isaac," Annie said. "They're just having a discussion among themselves. Now lie down and go to sleep."

But I couldn't sleep. I kept thinking about that baby, and I got madder and madder. It was so wrong, it was so unfair, everything that had happened—losing the mill and being driven out of our homes and pregnant women and old men having to walk all this distance. It was terrible and it made me furious. I lay there with my guts knotted and my hands clenched. I tried to tell myself to calm down, there wasn't any point in getting into a rage, but I couldn't stop it all from going round and round in my head—

Patterson and the mill, and Father out in the woods, and all of us camped in the wilderness with wolves howling around. Finally I gave up trying to sleep and got up. The wolves were still howling over at the north side of the meadow. I walked toward the sounds, skirting campfires and trying not to step on people sleeping in the dark. Finally I came to the edge of the clearing. The wolves were in the forest somewhere, back in the shadows. Every once in awhile I could see a little flashing pinprick of light, when the moon happened to catch their eyes. They went on howling.

"Damn you, shut up," I shouted. I bent over and picked up a stone from the meadow. "Get the hell out of here." I threw the stone off into the darkness. "Get out of here." I knelt down and searched the ground with my hand for stones. As fast as I could find them I flung them off into the woods, not bothering to stand up, but just kneeling and throwing and then scrambling around on my hands and knees for another stone. The clattering of the stones in the trees bothered them. They stopped howling, and I heard them moving around and then they were gone.

I went on kneeling there in the dark. It didn't make any sense to be fighting wolves and going hungry and beating along that overgrown road—for what? To go back to Connecticut and spend the rest of my life behind a plow on Uncle John's farm? All of a sudden I wished I'd gone off into the woods with Father. Maybe Patterson's Rangers really would be disbanded in a little while. Maybe we'd get the mill back. Maybe the Pennamites wouldn't bother us anymore after that. Wasn't it worth trying? Wasn't it worth fighting just a little for? But who would look after Annie and Little Isaac? I couldn't find an answer, so I went back to our fire and lay down and went to sleep.

For two more days we walked on. Most people were very low on food. Patterson had come up so suddenly that they hadn't time to collect very much. There was a story going around about one woman who had three or four children. The baby died, and she cooked it and fed it to the other children. I don't know if the story was true, but a lot of people swore it was. People were snatching at berries and chewing buds on bushes as they went along. I kept an eye out for small animals' trails where I might be able to set a snare, but with this many people tramping along the animals were scared off. I just didn't know what we were going to do. We were going slower than I'd figured. We came to a couple of more streams but by the time everybody had forded them the bottom was all roiled up and there wasn't any point in trying to fish. If it had been just me and Annie and Little Isaac I could have managed to find food. But with five hundred people marching along smashing things down and scaring off the game there wasn't much hope. The only thing we could do was push on as fast as we could and hope that once we crossed the Delaware and got into New York, they'd have some food to share with us. After that it wouldn't be so bad. We wouldn't be in the forest anymore, we'd be in farming country, and we'd be able to beg enough to keep us going until we got back to Uncle John's. We might even be able to get rides in people's wagons as we went along. At least there would be real roads.

Our food ran out on the fifth day. At noon, when we stopped to rest, I told Annie, "I'm going to try to find something to eat. Maybe I can get a couple of squirrels or something."

"With your bare hands?"

"Maybe I can get one with a stone. Maybe I'll find a berry patch. You just go along with the others. I can easily catch up to you by nightfall."

"Don't get lost," she said.

"Pretty hard to lose this bunch."

I walked off the old road into the woods. The first thing I did was to shove a half dozen stones into my pockets. Then I found a piece of dried oak branch lying on the ground. I broke the small end of it off to use as a club, and began moving through the woods away from the road, watching for animal signs. It was going to be hard to kill an animal with stones and a club, but it was possible. And there was always the chance of finding some eggs or nuts or even a wounded deer that had got away from a hunter and couldn't run. Or maybe I'd come across a pool where I could catch some fish.

I knew I wasn't going to find anything near the road, though. So I walked on pretty quickly, moving my eyes around—up for birds' nests and squirrels, down for signs of animal trails. And I was going along like that when I heard somebody say my name just as clear as could be. "Ben."

I stopped dead. The sound was so real I could hardly believe it wasn't. But, of course, I was just hearing things. When you're hungry and tired funny things happen. So I went on, and then I heard it again: "Ben."

I stopped again. There was silence. I started to put my foot forward and it came again, "Ben," and I knew I wasn't hearing things and I spun around.

Joe Mountain was standing by a tree behind me. He was carrying a rifle and he was looking at me to see what I would do.

"Joe," I said. We stood there looking at each other, neither one of us moving.

"You still mad at me, Ben?" he said.

It made me feel bad to hear him say that. He was the one who had the right to be mad, because of me

trying to get him to come back and be Father's slave
the night of the flood. "I'm not mad at you, Joe," I
said. Then we raced toward each other and threw
our arms around each other and hugged.

"Where have you been, Joe?"

"In the woods. Living in those caves." He
reached into his pocket and pulled out something
wrapped up in a piece of oilcloth. "Here," he said. It
was a piece of venison. "I guess you're pretty hungry."

"I guess I am," I said. I sat down on the ground
and began to chew on the meat. Joe sat there and
watched me, his gun lying across his legs. I knew I
should save part of the meat for Annie and Little
Isaac, but I ate half of it before I could stop myself.
Finally I stopped, though, and wrapped the rest of it
back up in the oilcloth. "I have to save some for the
others," I said. "How did you know we were here?"

He laughed. "Everybody in the whole world
knows you're here. You can't walk five hundred people through the woods without everybody knowing
it for ten miles around."

"I guess it wasn't any secret," I said. "Patterson
didn't make any secret of it."

"Listen, Ben. Patterson's going to leave Wilkes-
Barre."

"What?"

"He's going to leave. The order came down from

the Assembly. That's what I came to tell you."

"How do you know that? Who says it?"

"Well, you know, Ben, there's maybe two dozen Connecticut men living in those caves up above the valley. Maybe even more than that."

"What are you living on?"

"Oh, there's plenty to eat. We set snares, and we still have some powder and ball. It's even easier than that. There's a lot of rye growing on some of those upland farms where Patterson ran the people out and put Pennamites in. We just sneak in at night and do some harvesting."

"And Patterson is leaving?"

"The order came down for the Rangers to disband. He'll leave when they do. There's too many of us out in the woods who'd dearly love to get a shot at him. I'd do it myself—I wouldn't be afraid to."

"But how do you *know* they're going to disband?"

"There's still a few Connecticut people in the valley—Patterson didn't have time to run them all out. They hear things whenever they go into Wilkes-Barre."

"Is somebody living in our mill?"

"Some Pennamite from Easton."

"Boy, that makes me mad."

"He won't be there long, after the Rangers are gone."

"What are you going to do?"

"When the Rangers go we'll come down out of the woods and drive the Pennamites out."

"Have the Pennamites been up there trying to catch you?"

"Patterson came out with a detachment of Rangers once. It didn't amount to anything. We just sat off in the woods and let them come on up the road, and then we took a few shots at them and it scared them off. They couldn't get up into the woods on horseback and they sure weren't going to come in there on foot."

"Did you shoot, too, Joe?"

"Sure."

"Did you kill anybody?"

"Sure," he said. "Well, I think maybe I did. It was kind of hard to tell what you were hitting."

"What did it feel like?"

"It didn't feel like anything. It wasn't anything."

All of a sudden I realized something queer. Now it was Joe who was going to grow up free and be his own man; and it was me who was going to be somebody's slave. It sure was strange. Joe had to leave the mill to be free, but I couldn't be free without it. An awful feeling came over me, like being stuck in the mud and sinking down deeper. I knew I deserved it, for trying to keep Joe a slave that time. Still, it felt horrible to know that for all the rest of my life I would have to do what somebody else wanted me to do; knowing that I could never really decide anything for myself, and anything I built would be for somebody else. "Joe, what'll you do if you drive the Pennamites out?"

"Oh, I guess there'll be an extra piece of land left over somewhere. There's enough dead who won't be putting in any claims. I could get my own farm somewhere. The other thing I was thinking about, there's one of the fellows up there who's a blacksmith and going to set up in Wilkes-Barre. Maybe I might apprentice to him."

"You've got to get the Pennamites out first, though."

"Oh, we'll get them out. We're not scared to fight."

And suddenly I knew that I was going back to Wilkes-Barre. I just couldn't stand not to. I couldn't stand never having anything of my own, never being my own man. I knew I'd be back.

I stood up. "I have to go. I have to catch up with the rest. But tell Father I'll be back. Tell Father I'm going to see Annie and Little Isaac safe into Connecticut. And then I'll be back. Tell Father not to get anyone for the mill in my place. Tell Father I'll help him finish it when I get back."

"I'll tell him," Joe said.

We shook hands and I trotted toward the old road,

feeling better than I had for a long, long, time.

And that was the way it went. It took us three more days to get to the Delaware River and then across. After that it was easier. The whole crowd began to split up, going off in their own directions toward where they had friends or relatives. We headed on through New York, stopping in little towns along the way. Sometimes I could get a day or two's work, which would earn us some food, and then we'd go on again. It took us about a week to get from the Delaware to the Hudson. We crossed the Hudson at the town of Hudson and two days later we were at Uncle John's.

I stayed there for about four weeks, seeing to it that Annie and Little Isaac were going to be properly settled, and helping Uncle John get in his corn. Then in the middle of August I started back for Wilkes-Barre. It was hard to say good-bye; I didn't know when I'd see them all again. But I left, and ten days later I walked back into the mill. Father was in the mill yard splitting some shingles. He'd got the walls up, but no roof yet. He stopped working when he saw me. "I'd about given up on you, Ben," he said, sort of smiling. Then he hugged me.

"You knew I'd come back, Father."

He grinned again. "I figured you might."

It had worked out just the way Joe Mountain had

said. The Rangers were disbanded on June 1st, and on July 23rd the men had come down out of the woods and driven the rest of the Pennamites out. There had been some fighting, but nothing like the old massacre. And so we had won. Of course it took a lot of lawyers' talk to straighten out the property rights so that we could keep what we'd won. But what a lot of grief had gone into it.

There really isn't much more to tell. Wilkes-Barre grew. We put up the sawmill to go along with the grist mill. The countryside was prosperous, business was good, and we began building up a surplus of flour to sell. This led us into bringing in other things to sell, too: sugar and whiskey and molasses and such, until finally we had a store. About that time Father went back to Connecticut to pay a visit, and especially to see Annie, because she was going to marry a farmer back there whose wife had died. He brought Little Isaac back with him. Annie hated to let him go, but she knew it was better for him. Out in Wilkes-Barre he had a future; in Connecticut he had none.

Finally Father put up a house at the back of our land, up above the high meadow, where we could look down on the river and the mills. We turned the old house into a store. Over the years we cleared off nearly a hundred acres and put in our own wheat. By

the time 1800 came around, and I was just thirty
with a family of my own, we were business men more
than anything else. Isaac—we stopped calling him
Little Isaac when he got to be six feet tall—was running the farm, I was running the mills, and Father
was tending the store and taking care of trade. So I
must say, we got to be pretty prosperous.

And Joe Mountain. Well, after the Pennamites
left he took over a farm that had no claims on it, and
began to grow some rye. I figured that wouldn't last
very long, and it didn't. Joe just didn't have the tem-
perament for anything so slow as farming. Next he
apprenticed himself to the blacksmith. That lasted
around six months, but finally he got fed up with it.
He said, "It's too much like being a nigger all over
again. I just don't like doing what other people tell
me."

"What are you going to do?"

"Go trapping. Go up into the mountains after
beaver pelts. There's a lot of money in it."

"You mean go and live in the woods all winter?"

"Sure," he said. "That doesn't scare me any."

"I didn't figure it would."

I didn't see him much after that. Every once in
a while he'd turn up in Wilkes-Barre and we'd get
together for a day or two. Mostly, though, he was
either out in the woods with some other trappers, or

in New York or Philadelphia selling his pelts.

But I never forgot him, either, and especially I never forgot the night of the flood, when we sat up in the high meadow and I tried to talk him into coming back to be our nigger. For years afterward I thought about that: and I guess the only lesson I found in it is that it's hard as hell to spend your life never belonging to yourself. No one wants to be a slave, whether it's the kind Joe Mountain was with a master who owned him, or the kind I almost got to be—having to work for somebody else with no chance of building something for myself. Most people are no different from Joe Mountain or me: they can't stand being slaves, and they'll do anything to get out of it. They'll even take a chance on getting themselves killed for it. And the other thing I figured about that is, it doesn't much matter whether you're white or black or Indian or a mixture, the way Joe Mountain was; to be a slave feels about the same for everybody.

How Much of This Book Is True?

Finding out exactly what happened in the past is always difficult; nonetheless, this story is based entirely on historical facts as we have been able to ascertain them. Of course, the Buck family is made up, but people like Ben, Joe Mountain and the rest did live in the Wyoming Valley at that time. And the dialogue is made up, too. We have used modern speech, partly to make the story easier to understand, and partly because we don't really know how people in those days talked.

But all of the main events happened just as we described them. Wilkes-Barre was as we have pictured it, and there was a mill like the Bucks' on Mill Creek. There was a terrible massacre of Connecticut settlers by the British and their Indian and Tory allies, in which hundreds of people were murdered for no good reason. Alexander Patterson was a real person, and unhappily, he was just the sort of person we have made him out to be. The flood happened just that way, and the part about the men living out in caves is true as well. Sadly, so was the long trek out of the valley by the women and children. Many people died on this journey, and it is reported—as we have said—that one woman did indeed cook a child who had died to feed to her other children.

In the end, Wilkes-Barre grew and prospered—although only a few years ago, the Susquehanna again rose over its banks and flooded thousands out of their houses, just as it had done in Ben Buck's time. There is a historical museum in Wilkes-Barre, and if you happen to live nearby, you can go there and look up all the details of the events you read about in this book.